MALCOLM
DIRTY ACES MC

LANE HART
D.B. WEST

COPYRIGHT

This book is a work of fiction. The characters, incidents, and dialogue were created from the authors' imagination and are not to be construed as real. Any resemblance to actual people or events is coincidental.

The authors acknowledge the copyrighted and trademarked status of various products within this work of fiction.

© 2020 Editor's Choice Publishing

All Rights Reserved.

Only Amazon has permission from the publisher to sell and distribute this title.

This book or any portion thereof may not be reproduced or used in any manner whatsoever without the express written permission of the publisher except for the use of brief quotations in a book review.

Editor's Choice Publishing

P.O. Box 10024

Greensboro, NC 27404

Edited by Angela Snyder
Cover by Melissa Gill Designs

WARNING: THIS BOOK IS NOT SUITABLE FOR ANYONE UNDER 18. IT CONTAINS STRONG LANGUAGE, VIOLENCE AND GRAPHIC SEX SCENES.

PLAYLIST

Five Finger Death Punch - *Bad Company*
Finger Eleven - *Paralyzer*
Audioslave - *I Am the Highway*
AC/DC - *Thunderstruck*
Lewis Capaldi - *Bruises*
AWOLNATION - *Not Your Fault*
AC/DC - *Highway to Hell*
Aerosmith - *Angel*

SYNOPSIS

While Malcolm Hyde may look like your very own personal Jesus, he's anything but a saint. Covered in tattoos and leather, he's a smoking hot biker and nothing but trouble.

As the president of the Dirty Aces MC, Malcolm is known for being cold and calculating. One bad decision – getting into business with the wrong person – is all it takes to bring down the entire MC. It's happened before to his predecessor, which is why Malcolm refuses to let it happen again on his watch. He doesn't trust anyone except for the few men who wear the same ace of spades patch on their back.

And that's exactly why he doesn't ever take his eyes off of me – the new girl. I never intended to make an enemy out of Malcolm or the MC when I was sent to steal everything I could from them.

After Malcolm finds out what I've been doing, he's furious and shows no mercy until I spill all of my secrets, ones that could very well end my life. That's when he makes me a surprising offer – he's willing to take care of all of my problems, and the only thing he's asking for in return is for me to completely surrender myself to him.

Spending two weeks in bed with a bad boy biker sounds more like a reward than a punishment.

There's just one little catch – once he claims my body, there's no guarantee he won't steal my heart too.

CHAPTER ONE

Malcolm Hyde

"Good news, prez. We've got five clubs up and down the east coast who would give their left nut to patch over," Nash says when he walks into the chapel and finds me sitting alone.

I take a deep pull from my cigarette and let the smoke roll out from my lips slowly. "So?" I ask him as I lean back in my chair at the head of the Dirty Aces' long wooden meeting table, my boots propped up on the corner, crossed at the ankle.

"So, everyone else is on board with expanding. Now is as good a time as any, right?" he explains, plopping down in his usual chair to my right.

"Careful, brother. I can practically see the dollar signs dancing in your eyes," I tell my VP with a raspy chuckle.

"Who doesn't like a little extra cash in their pocket every month?" he responds with a smirk. "But it's not just about the money.

It's about the power and the prestige, finally putting our club on the map."

"Prestige? Seriously?" I scoff.

Don't get me wrong. I'm all about more cash, more respect, and more power. Nash is right. Who doesn't want to have an abundance of those things, especially someone like me? I grew up so poor my piece of shit mother had me holding up cardboard signs begging for food and loose change at busy intersections from the time I was old enough to stand on two feet. After you've been truly hungry, desperate for a half-eaten cheeseburger someone tosses out their window, you don't ever forget that shit. That's why I'm so tight with my earnings now. I wear the same boots and torn jeans that I've had since I started prospecting – that was long before money started coming in from the Dirty Aces' gambling and drug enterprises hand over fist two years ago. Those memories of a constant gnawing ache in my empty stomach are why I still live in a one-bedroom beach cottage, drive a five-year-old bike, and put every penny into savings like I'm preparing for the apocalypse.

Never. Again.

Never again will I have to be a beggar on the streets or go to sleep hungry. That's the promise I made to myself after I turned sixteen and got my first job slinging pizza dough and delivering late night pies to stoners. Not only did I earn a wage, but one of the perks was getting to eat for free whenever I wanted, something that was a foreign fucking concept since my mother preferred booze or meth to feeding us.

"Look, man," Nash starts once I finish my smoke and put it out in the glass ashtray on the table. His knee is bouncing nervously, a clear indicator that he's uncomfortable with my silence. He knows I've been trying to avoid this conversation like the plague. "I get that the shit with Lowell fucked you up. It fucked us all up."

"Thanks for that newsflash, Captain Obvious," I mutter when he brings up the recent betrayal of one of our brothers. Lowell was stealing a shit ton of money from the club for months without any of us having a goddamn clue.

"You're convinced that we can't trust anyone outside of our circle, and maybe not everyone in it completely. But thinking like that is only going to hold us back from taking the Dirty Aces to the next level, becoming...more."

"Yeah, but why exactly do we need more?" I ask him. "Shit's great the way it is."

"Because growing is a sign of success."

"You sound like some shady CEO pushing a pyramid scheme when you say shit like that," I point out when I lower the soles of my boots back down to the floor and rest my elbows on the table. "Who the hell are you trying to impress, Nash? Ellie isn't coming back, man. It's been what? Over two years? And even if she did, having a few new charters isn't shit compared to the mountains of dough her daddy keeps her swimming in."

"Fuck you," he grits out through clenched teeth after I knowingly took aim and hit his sore spot. Shoving his chair back to shoot to his feet, he slams both of his palms down on the table in front of me. "None of this is about her, asshole! It's about what's best for the goddamn club. And you may be the president, but this isn't a dictatorship. You don't even have veto power. That's why I'm done waiting. Next time we meet, I'm bringing it to the table for a vote."

"Good for you," I grumble as I give him a dismissive wave.

Nash turns around and stomps out, slamming the door behind him like a toddler.

Hell, I know fighting the expansion is a lost cause. I've put off the damn vote as long as possible, but there's no way the other guys will say no. They all want the power and the money because it'll mean more pussy, which is pretty much the only fucking thing they care about.

But there's one thing that is more important to me than the increase in revenue or status, and that's loyalty.

You can't put a fucking price tag on that shit. Hell, it might be the only thing in this business that's truly priceless.

After one of our own brothers stabbed us in the back, I'm not too thrilled about opening our doors and letting in strangers. One wrong step and we could end up right back where we were a few years ago when the former Ace of Spades MC was literally burned to the ground for getting into business with the wrong people.

Now that I'm in charge, I won't ever let that shit happen again. This MC is all I fucking have, and nothing and no one is going to take it away from me.

CHAPTER TWO

Naomi Dawson

Despite the fact that all four windows of my ancient Chevy Malibu are rolled down, it's still too hot to sleep. Late June in Sea Breeze is the equivalent of a day in hell, except I doubt even hell is this muggy and humid, the salty air so thick you can almost grab it. I try rolling to my other side, facing the passenger side of the car in my reclined driver seat, but it's no use. Sleep isn't going to happen again tonight.

I miss my soft, cozy bed.
I miss my shower and clothes.
I miss...being home.
But at the moment, two linebacker-sized goons are sitting in an SUV right outside the driveway, waiting for me to return so that they can snatch me up.
Screw that and screw them.

Eventually, they'll get tired of waiting and leave. Probably. Maybe.

If I were smart, I would haul my ass right out of town and never look back.

Too bad I only have ten dollars to my name and can't even afford a full tank of gas at the moment. Sooner or later, I will also have to come out of hiding to go back to work or I'm going to get fired. *Sorry, but I can't come in again tonight because my father's goons are after me* won't go over well with my boss, Nancy. She's cranky and menopausal, working twelve-hour shifts on her feet managing slack-asses and serving guests in a greasy diner that's open all night, so I can't really blame her for having a piss poor attitude. God knows I would be snippy too if I end up working there for the next twenty years of my life.

I'm so busy thinking about how much shit I'm going to be in at work when I finally return that I don't even realize I'm no longer alone until someone's fingers are digging into the back of my short blonde hair. They give a harsh, sudden, sharp tug that causes something in my neck to pop.

Oh crap. Crap, crap, crap!

Screaming does no good since I'm parked in a closed used car lot, yet I still give it a shot, screaming for help as I'm yanked backward all the way out the open window none too gently. Squeezing through the tight space was actually nothing compared to hitting the pavement on my ass and being dragged across it as I dig my nails into the big hand to pry it from my hair.

"Stop it! Stop! Put me down, you fucking bastard!" I screech at my kidnapper.

His free hand slams across my face with a hard whap that leaves my cheek throbbing. "Keep clawing at me and I'll bring you in without a pulse!" the giant warns me before I'm picked up under my arms and tossed into the cargo area of his SUV. He slams the door on me; and before I can find a latch to open it back up, the sound of the locks engage just as the SUV lunges forward, peeling out of the gravel parking lot.

"The scrawny bitch made me bleed!" my kidnapper has the audacity to complain to someone, most likely the guy driving him. It's dark and I can't see their faces from two rows back, so I climb over the back of the seat, moving closer to a door. Since it's a suburban or some other big SUV, I still have another seat to hurdle over.

"Told you that you should've put on your leather gloves."

"No shit. She's lucky I didn't rip her head off!"

I've got one leg over the middle row when the kidnaper yells, "Get your ass back or I'll put a bullet in you, cunt!"

After I hear the clicking sound of his gun being cocked, I slowly ease down into the back seat.

"She's a feisty one. I don't mind when they fight back," the driver says as we roll through the city. The numerous streetlights of our tourist beach town allow his eyes to find me in the rear-view. "Wonder how much boss wants for her."

The kidnapper scoffs. "That's his daughter. She won't go cheap. Heard she owes him twenty grand."

"Too bad I only have ten in savings. I'd gladly cough it all up for that ass."

"Who knows?" the kidnapper tells his buddy. "Boss might loan her out to you."

"Yeah, maybe so."

If I had any food in my stomach, it would probably be on the seat next to me by now after listening to them talk about me in such a horrible, crude way. Some people might think they were just trying to scare me by talking about me like I'm an object and not a human being, but I know enough about my estranged father to be certain that it's not just talk.

A few weeks ago, I stole something from him. Something I can't ever get back. And since I won't ever be able to pay back the twenty thousand dollars or return the historical memento he was so proud to own, there's no clue what he'll do to me.

There's one thing I'm certain of – he won't show me any mercy just because we share similar DNA.

∼

"Naomi! My silly, stupid girl. What were you thinking, gumdrop?" Harold Cox asks once I'm standing before him. Most people probably think he changed his name to make it as disgusting as possible, but the truth is his parents must have known he would turn out to be a dick. I mean, his lard ass is actually sitting on a custom-made throne in the middle of his mansion. His minions, the elite, upper crust of the city along with various crooked politicians are milling about the three-story southern plantation house drinking, smoking, and laughing while I await my punishment.

"I'm sorry," I tell him meekly as I fidget with my fingers in front of me. I really am sorry, though it's only for getting caught, not for the actual act of stealing from him.

"Sorry?" he snaps. "Sorry isn't going to bring back George Washington's original signature block, *is it*?"

That's right. My father, a man I've only seen a handful of times, is not only a mobster but a huge history buff.

"No," I whisper.

"No, it's not!" he yells, causing some of the guests to pause momentarily in the middle of their conversations about taking over the world before going back to their good time.

"I'll get the money, and-and then I'll buy it back," I assure him, even though we both know I'm full of shit. That signature is long gone.

"There's no amount of money that will replace what I've lost, what you *stole* from me when you came into my home as a guest," he replies calmly as he smooths back what's left of his thinning, pale blond hair. And I know he's super pissed if he's no longer yelling but primping. His swollen chest is puffing rapidly up and down, and his chubby face is the brightest of red, looking like he's seconds away from a heart attack.

"Then how...how can I make it up to you, *daddy*?" I ask, tacking on the title I've never used before to try and invoke any tiny smidgeon of sympathy he may still possess in his soul for me, his illegitimate daughter.

"Oh, you'll never be able to make this up to me, gumdrop," he says without hesitation. "Now I'm just trying to decide how I should punish you."

Great.

"One option is to simply sell you to the highest bidder..."

"What?" I exclaim.

"I always knew you were a gold-digger just like your mother. If you're going to act like a conniving whore, using me for money, I have no choice but to treat you like one. How much do you think she'll go for at auction, Dirk?" he asks one of the goons who brought me in – the driver who I now can see is completely bald and the size of two normal-sized men, if one was sitting on the other's shoulders.

"Ah, not much, boss. Renting her out a night at a time like the whore she is could be more economical for you in the long run," he offers with a smirk in my direction.

"Huh. Maybe," my father easily agrees with the disgusting man. Rubbing his chin, Harry adds, "Or I could use her to kill two birds with one stone. I know a fucker riding a very high horse that needs to be taken down a few notches..."

"Yes! That's what you should do. Let me help you take him down!" I exclaim. Anything, *any-fucking-thing*, is better than being *sold* to a different man every night!

"Eh, it's a big decision. I think I need to sleep on it," Harry says as he grabs the arm rests and struggles to his feet. "I'll let you know tomorrow."

"Tomorrow?" I shout. "Wh-what am I supposed to do until then?"

"Wait," he replies.

"Wait?"

"Yes. Right there. Don't move. Dirk is going to keep an eye on you. And if you try to leave, we'll just go ahead and go with his idea of renting you out by the night or by the hour, I don't really care which."

Great. That's just fucking great.

So much for expecting any leniency from my dear old dad.

CHAPTER THREE

Malcolm

When I bang on the table to bring the meeting to order, all of the gathered members of the Dirty Aces shut up immediately. I glance over at my VP, Nash, who is still shuffling through a stack of papers until he looks up and gives me a nod.

"All right, fellas, I'm going to make this quick so we can get out to the boat and get to work tonight," I tell them. When I look down the table and see Fiasco's looking down at his crotch, I stop and stare at him until he looks up at me. His pale blue eyes look vaguely confused, and he swipes a hand through his sun-bleached blond hair before giving an embarrassed grin. "Something interesting down there, big guy?" I ask him.

"Aw, shit, sorry prez. I had an itch, that's all," Fiasco says as his cheeks redden.

"You know staring at it won't make it better, right?" Wirth asks. Reaching a tattooed hand up to scratch his own shaven head, Wirth adds, "You gotta get in there and really dig if you want it to feel better."

"He was looking to see if anything was moving down there!" Devlin howls with laughter. Devlin and Fiasco are the biggest guys on our crew and are both tasked with doing any 'heavy lifting', or bare-knuckle work, that comes along.

"I was not!" Fiasco protests. "Besides, even if the itch was the bugs again, they can be really hard to see!"

"The bugs?" Silas, our secretary, groans. He turns his deep-set dark eyes to me with a grimace. "Tell me that dumb bastard doesn't have crabs! For fuck's sake, he lounges around here with his dick out half the time!"

"It's not the bugs!" Fiasco protests again. "I shaved and then it was really hot today out at the new mall we're building. None of you would know shit about actual hard work. Even Wirth over here just drives the heavy equipment. Dev and I are the only ones who actually swing a hammer!"

"Because that's about all you're good for," Silas sneers.

"Hey, that's enough," I shut them all up in an instant when I raise my voice. "Fiasco, do what you need to do and shut the fuck up. The rest of you ignore him. Now, Nash and I have been talking a lot about doing some patch-overs lately to get some new blood into the crew. He's been doing some research on some other local MCs, and he's come up with some potential candidates."

"Potential is the keyword, here," Nash interjects.

"Before we agree to do any patch overs or even vote on anything, I want to meet these guys. Let's bring them here, pour a few gallons of booze down their throats and offer them a buffet of pussy to see what they're really made of."

"Sounds like a damn good time," Wirth laughs. "I don't think any of our prospects would turn down that sort of opportunity, prez."

"I'll set it up," Nash agrees.

"Next month," I add. When he sighs heavily at me putting it off,

MALCOLM

I explain to him and the other guys why I want to wait. "First, we need time to hire a PI to scope them out."

"A private investigator for all five groups? You really think that's necessary?" Nash questions.

"Yeah, I do."

"Are we gonna weed out the ones with criminal records now too?" Devlin snorts. "'Cause that would be all of us. I know you're paranoid, boss, but you really need to chill the fuck out."

"I don't give a shit about their criminal records," I argue. "I just want to know who they associate with, the people in their circles. Make sure there's no law enforcement or mafia-types pulling their strings."

"Fine," Nash agrees on a sigh. "We'll vet them for a few weeks before we bring them to the boat to party."

"Meeting adjourned," I say with a slam of the gavel, ready to drop the topic.

The guys get up to leave, making their way to the door. On his way around the table, Silas slaps my shoulder and says, "No offense, man, but how long has it been since you spent some time with the Booty Call Squad? You're wound tight and are gonna snap if you don't find a way to relax soon."

"You should worry more about yourself and less about me and my dick," I warn him before he throws his head back and walks out chuckling.

~

Naomi

I'M NOT sure what my father has against Malcolm Hyde and I don't really care. From my limited research on the biker, which consisted of asking the cooks if they had heard of him once I returned to work last night, I know he's the president of the Dirty Aces motorcycle gang, and that's about it. I seriously doubt that he's a good, honest guy, especially since the first thing anyone said about the Dirty Aces was that they were a bunch of shady drug dealers.

My mom died of an overdose ten years ago when I was only eleven, so I have no qualms about stealing from the guys peddling that crap on the streets. Not that she was ever much of a mother to me before she left this world. If not for my grandparents, I would've ended up in foster homes. I'm thankful to Gram and Gramps with every breath and still miss them like crazy.

For a year now, I've been on my own with only one relative still breathing – my asshole father. Harry's never been there for birthday parties or holidays. He wasn't the kind of dad to even bother sending a card in the mail. I've never asked for anything from him, and he's never given me anything other than the money I desperately needed a few weeks ago when I stole from his personal collection of 'historical artifacts'.

Now, I have no choice but to make amends by snooping on the Dirty Aces and their president, in particular, as well as trying to embezzle as much as I can while I pretend to be a hardworking employee.

The first step in this plan of his requires me to quit my waitressing job and try to get hired onto the Aces' gambling cruise ship. It's not like they have a help wanted sign up or anything on their clubhouse. I doubt a gang that deals in illegal activities ever asks strangers to come work for them.

Which is why getting onto the stupid boat may be the hardest part of Harry's idiotic idea. He was confident that all I have to do is show a little skin and bat my eyes to seal the deal. I have my doubts, but I'd rather take a chance with these bikers than face my father's 'alternatives'.

I'm not a virgin or anything close to it. But I don't actively flirt with men to take advantage of them. Occasionally, I've taken easy opportunities, snatching up a wallet or cell phone from a guy when the situation presented itself. When the power company was threatening to leave Gram and I in the dark right after Gramps died, I didn't have any other options. Times were tight, so I did what I had to do without any regrets. It's not like I spent the money on a jet ski or a vacation. Those sorts of luxuries are for the rich, not burger slinging waitresses who work the graveyard shift to pay the bills.

At least now that I have a deal with Harry, I'm able to sleep in my own bed, shower and change clothes whenever I like. For a while, those simple things were *my* indulgences.

Freshly washed with a face full of makeup and my short, blonde hair styled with beach waves, I parallel park my Malibu in an empty spot right in front of the old warehouse that has been converted into a huge pool hall, bar, and garage. The sun is still high in the sky, and I'm guessing a shady place like this doesn't start getting busy until late at night. Grabbing one of my printed resumes, I climb out of my car, toss my keys in my purse and strut right inside the building like I belong, even if I already know I'm going to look out of place in my white lace sundress. It's the sexiest thing I own, and I'm certain that I need all the help I can get in that department.

Compared to the bright summer day outside, inside the long hall is dark and empty with a few florescent bulbs hanging from the wall over each pool table. There's a well-polished wooden bar with stools at the front that are all vacant. The only person in the room is a buff, blond man wearing a leather vest behind the bar. He's busy pulling a lever to fill up a glass with a yellow liquid that is no doubt beer even though it's only lunchtime. His head turns to look at me, and he stares for so long his glass overflows.

That's probably a good sign that my dress is working.

"Hi," I say to him with a wave of my resume. "You may want to..." I gesture to his glass, and he finally breaks eye contact with me to look down.

"Oh shit!" he exclaims as he lets go of the lever and jumps backward. He doesn't seem too concerned with the mess on the floor, not bothering to grab a towel. He simply strolls in my direction, putting the full glass to his lips and guzzling down half the beverage. "What's up?" he asks, licking his lips to wipe off the foam and revealing a tongue piercing.

"I'm sorry to just drop in like this. It doesn't look like you're open yet, but I wanted to see if you're hiring and drop off my resume."

"Your resume?" he repeats with a grin. "Does this look like the type of joint that gives a shit about resumes?"

After another quick glance around the room, I meet his gaze again. "Ah, no, I guess not."

The less these guys know about me the better, so I ball up the piece of paper and then shoot it basketball style into the nearest trash can.

"She shoots, she scores!" the man announces, adding a crowd roar.

"I'm Naomi," I say, holding out my hand for him to take when he's close enough.

"Fiasco," he responds, switching his beer to his left to quickly shake my palm with his right hand.

"Pardon?" I ask in confusion.

"My name's Phillip, but everyone calls me Fiasco," he explains. "Pretty self-explanatory."

"Oh, okay," I reply. "It's nice to meet you, Fiasco. So, you're one of the Dirty Aces?" I guess when I see the words printed on a patch sewn to his vest.

"Sure am. How can I help you?"

"Are you hiring by chance?" I ask while giving him my best pleading look, practically batting my blue eyes that are several shades darker than his.

"Sorry, babe," he replies before taking another gulp to finish off his beer and then slamming the empty glass down on the bar. "You might be a stunner, but we don't have any openings for jailbait," he mutters with a grin as disappointment falls heavy on my shoulders. "And, girl, no lie, I'm doing you a favor, because your sweet little ass would get eaten alive by our customers. Seriously, I left a box of doughnuts on the bar one night, and some psycho ate the whole thing. I mean, like, the actual cardboard and all. They'd treat you the same." He takes one long last look at my tan legs hanging out of my dress before he shakes his head and starts strolling down a back hallway.

"Wait," I shout, hurrying to catch up to him in my wedge sandals, unable to accept defeat so soon. If I can't find a way to get hired, I'm screwed. Worse than screwed. *Anything* is better than what my father has in store for me if I fail. "Please," I say when I grab Fiasco's bare arm to make him stop and listen to me. "I'll do anything — waitress, hostess, wash dishes. There's got to be *something* I can do on the Dirty Aces' gambling boat, right? I mean...I'm a hard worker and-and I'm desperate."

"Desperate, huh?" he asks before his tongue makes a salacious swipe along his bottom lip, revealing the barbell piercing in the center again.

"Yes, I am," I affirm, inwardly cringing at how pathetically low I've sunk. I told myself I have to do whatever it takes to pay off the debt I owe to Harry, but saying it and doing it are two very different things. My stomach drops and bile burns my throat at just the *thought* of what he threatened to do to me if I don't get him his money by the end of the month. Nothing Fiasco can do to me would be worse than what's in store if I fail. Time's running out, so I'll have to just suck it up. Besides, I could do a lot worse than the big, blond biker with a tongue stud. Knowing just how furious Harry would be if he found out I fooled around with one of the Dirty Aces, who he apparently loathes, is another bonus. My father loves to remind me that I'm already a whore like my mother. Maybe I am. Still, no matter what it takes to pay him back, I don't regret it. I'd steal from him to get the cash all over again, if given the choice.

"Do you have an ID that says you're at least twenty-one?" Fiasco asks, not asking if I am of age but if I can pretend to be.

"Yes!" I agree, pulling out my real ID from the purse on my

shoulder to hold up in front of his face. At least I don't need to lie about this.

"All right, sweet cheeks," Fiasco says as I put my license away. "Let's go see if you can put your money where your mouth is."

"Right now?" I ask.

"Right now."

"And if I...put my money where my mouth is, does that mean you'll give me a job?" I ask while following along behind him down the hallway to a small storage room where cases of beer are stacked up in rows several feet high.

"Fuck yeah, I'll get you on the boat," he agrees, shutting the door behind me and resting his back against it. "After we're finished up here, all you need to do is come back tonight at eight in a black cocktail dress," he tells me while eyeing my white one that glows in the dark room. "The shorter and the more your tits show, the better your waitressing tips will be."

"Great, thank you so much!" I exclaim.

"Actions speak louder than words, babe," he says while his hand grabs my shoulder and pushes me down to the floor. "Get on your knees and show me just how thankful you really are."

CHAPTER FOUR

Naomi

Fiasco made good on his promise. At eight o'clock, he welcomed me aboard the *Pirate's Booty* in my short, black, sleeveless dress with the taste of him still on my lips even after three swigs of mouthwash.

It's not exactly a bad flavor. And under any other circumstance, I probably wouldn't have even minded getting him off with my mouth. It's just the shame of *why* I did it that's still haunting me, making me feel like a stranger in my own skin, doing things I wouldn't normally do if not for the anvil Harry is holding over my head. I had to get on my knees for *him*, not for myself, which makes me hate my biological father even more than I thought possible.

Still, I'm here, on the gambling boat, ready to take the next step in my plan of ripping off the Dirty Aces, and Malcolm Hyde specifically, any way possible to earn back twenty-thousand dollars. Or is it now twenty-one thousand thanks to Harry's ridiculously unfair but unavoidable interest rate?

The bartender, a squinty-eyed girl named Ronnie, spends about ten minutes training me on taking drink orders, filling them, and where to put the money once the customer pays since they deal solely in cash. That means it'll be easier than I thought to skim a little right off the top without anyone the wiser.

There aren't many gamblers on the boat tonight, but the ones I do serve are generous tippers. I've made a hundred bucks before the sun fully sets, which is way more than I usually make in an entire night at the diner.

I've just finished making the rounds and am taking a breather at the bar when a new man comes waltzing into the game room from a side entrance, looking like my very own personal Jesus with his wavy brown hair that brushes his shoulders. In jeans and a leather vest identical to Fiasco's, it becomes immediately clear that the guy is also a member of the Dirty Aces. After a notable hush falls over the room, everyone pausing in the middle of their card game or dice to turn and look at him, I start to think that this man isn't just any member of the MC but very likely their president.

After someone presses the imaginary play button and everybody goes back to what they were doing before his majesty entered, I whisper to Anika, the only other waitress who works weeknights, "Who is that?"

"Don't even think about it," she responds while chomping extra hard on her chewing gum. "Malcolm's a unicorn."

"A what?" I ask.

"A unicorn. Sure, he's pretty to look at and the most powerful man in town, but there's no chance in hell that you'll ever get to ride him. Seriously, the best thing you can do is pretend he's imaginary and go on with your life."

Wow. I knew Anika wasn't too thrilled about me dipping into her and the bartender's tips or whatever, but still, that's no reason to go full-on bitch so fast.

"Oh. Don't take it personally," she says with a wave of her hand, having apparently read my shocked face correctly. "Malcolm doesn't know we, his employees, exist, no matter how hard you flirt with him or try to get in his jeans. Believe me, I've tried and so has everyone else."

"Everyone else?" I ask.

"Oh yeah. On the weekends, we have another bartender and three other waitresses. Then there's the three girls who work at the pool hall. So, that's what, ten women counting me? Yeah, at least ten current employees of the Dirty Aces who have all tried and been shot down by Malcolm."

"He's turned down everyone?"

"Everyone," she says, blowing a small pink bubble and popping it. "There's a pool going if you want to throw in twenty bucks; but honestly, it'll just be a waste of money. It's up to eight hundred dollars, so thirty-two women have tried and failed to get their hands on Malcolm's dick."

"Wow," I mutter, unsure if that's just sad for the pathetic women or impressive that a man that hot has that kind of restraint. "Is he gay?" I whisper.

"No way to know for sure, of course, but I don't think so," Anika replies with a grin. "I've seen him checking me out before."

"Good for you, I guess. Thanks for the heads-up," I tell her.

"No problem," she says before she struts off to make the rounds on her customers.

After she's gone, I watch the ridiculously sexy man, who I can apparently never have, take a seat on one of the stools at the bar and plop down a stack of papers, placing his phone on top of them. He looks angry as he shoves his fingers roughly through the front of his thick locks to push them out of his face, huffing as if they intentionally hung in front of his eyes to piss him off. His thick, tattooed biceps flex with the movement, drawing my eye to them. I wouldn't mind running my own fingers through the waves either, having never dated a guy with long hair, or have those strong arms hold me down and take whatever they wanted from me...

Oh jeez! I have no clue where those naughty thoughts came from. I'm here to take care of business, not drool over some random man my father happens to hate. I cannot and will not get distracted from my goal of paying off my debt. The clock is ticking, and I need to get my ass moving.

Still, despite repeatedly telling myself to forget about Malcolm Hyde, I somehow find myself heading in his direction half an hour later, unable to resist getting a little closer to the sexy man in charge.

And as stupid as it may be, I can't help but hope Anika was wrong about him not wanting me.

Malcolm

It's going to take a gallon of whiskey to help me get through the club's end of the month accounting bullshit and the headache it's causing.

I fucking hate math.

It's my least favorite thing in the world. But after Lowell, one of our own damn guys, stole hundreds of thousands of dollars from the MC, I have no choice but to suck it up and take over the accounting. I'd rather be sitting back, smoking a joint while playing poker or blackjack with all the other guys on our gambling boat, but that's not going to happen tonight.

Having someone like me, a grumpy bastard who came from nothing and doesn't like to spend an unnecessary penny, do the books can be problematic for the club, because I want to cut out all sorts of shit that the guys love, like pay-per-view at the bar.

"Hey, it's Malcolm, right? Can I get you a beer?" a woman asks me sweetly while my head is bent over one of our beer vendors invoices. Ronnie, our bartender, and most of the waitresses know better than to bother me while I'm fucking working.

"No, but you can get me a fifth of whiskey," I say with a sigh since she's already interrupted.

"How much is a fifth?" she asks.

"For fuck's sake," I mutter when I finally lift my eyes to see which of our waitresses is seriously asking me that question. Well, that explains the problem. The skinny little blonde that I've never seen before looks too young to be holding a tray and serving alcohol. The last thing we need is a goddamn ABC violation. "Who the hell are you?" I ask her.

"Oh, I'm Naomi," she says with a smile.

"Where did you come from?"

"Sea Breeze, just north of here."

"No, honey. I don't care where the fuck you were born. I want to know how the fuck you got on my boat," I snap at her. "Who hired you?"

"Oh, um, Fiasco," she answers with her cheeks turning a bright shade of red.

"Of course he did," I mutter as I eye her from the top of her short blonde hair pushed behind her ears, down the curves of her tight, sleeveless black dress to the toes of her black strappy heels that wrap around her ankle. She's sexy as hell, sure, but way too young and innocent to be working in a Dirty Aces establishment. "How old are you? Show me your ID."

"I-I don't have my ID on me. It's back in the employee room though, in my purse," she responds.

"How old does your ID say you are? Your *real* one. And if you know what's good for you, you better not fucking lie to me," I warn her with a threatening glare.

Her blue eyes lined with long, thick, black lashes widen comically, making her look even more like an innocent teen model who got on the wrong damn boat.

"I'm twenty-one."

"Prove it," I tell her, spinning toward her in my barstool. When she continues to stand there in front of me, unmoving, I say, "Hustle, honey. I ain't got all day."

"Yes, sir," she responds. Sitting her round tray down on top of the counter next to me, she hurries off behind the bar to the employee lounge, stumbling in her heels like she doesn't have much experience wearing them.

A moment later, she comes running back, the small plastic ID card in her hand.

"Here," she says, panting and making me think of other ways to take her breath away, especially when I see her date of birth along with the watermark that tells me her license is the real deal.

"How long have you been working here?" I ask.

"Tonight's my first night."

"No shit," I huff. "Why don't you go find a job at Applebee's or some other family establishment tomorrow? You sure as shit don't belong here."

"Why do you say that?" she asks, giving me a little bit of attitude and drawing my attention to her pink, pouty lips that belong on a porn star.

Ignoring my dick's interest in her mouth, I tell her, "Look, honey. I don't have time to baby you every time somebody slaps your ass. And I sure as fuck won't be wasting the club's money on attorneys for sexual harassment lawsuits. Tonight's your last night."

Her front teeth bite down on her plump bottom lip and then she steps forward. Stroking her hands up both of my spread jean-covered thighs, she moves into the space between them. Her hips are so lean that she wedges them right on in until her flat stomach is rubbing up on my dick. "I'm not easily offended, and I promise I won't cause you any problems."

"Oh yeah?" I ask. "How do you plan to prove that?"

"However I need to," she says, not so subtly grinding against my hard bulge. "Just ask Fiasco."

Goddamn him for screwing everything that walks. I'm both surprised and a little pissed that he was able to convince a girl like Naomi to do him. But if there's one thing I know about the women who hang around the Dirty Aces' establishments, it's that they'll do anything for the right price, be it cash or dope.

"I'm not going to fuck you," I tell her, which is the honest to god truth. No matter how sexy she is or how many times she tries to push up on my dick, I don't screw the help. *Ever.* It's a hard and fast rule of mine ever since I've been in charge to avoid drama. All the other guys, except for Nash, who has his own reasons for abstaining, pass our girls around like they're toys, each taking a turn playing with them. Hell, sometimes two even bang one of them at the same time. Their motto is any pussy will do, while I'm a bit more selective. Not that I'm monogamous or anything of the sort. Back in town, I've got three women on speed dial who come for me and only me whenever I want them. Silas calls them my Booty Call Squad. Each knows about the others, so I'm not screwing around behind anyone's back. They're welcome to walk away and see other men whenever they want; but while they're fucking me, they keep that pussy on lockdown for me and only me. It comes at a high price to have convenient pussy, but doesn't it always?

Naomi is quiet for several seconds as my rejection sinks in. Eventually, she asks, "Then how do you want me to prove I'm not easily offended?"

Inspiration hits with an idea so fucked up that I'm willing to bet she would rather jump ship than go through with it. It's low, almost as low as Fiasco went, but all she has to do is decline and quit, which I'm certain she'll decide to do.

Reaching around her back with my left hand, I find her dress's zipper and slowly start to lower it, counting down the seconds before she jumps ship. "You're going to prove it by taking your dress off and finishing your shift wearing only what's underneath," I tell her. "If you make it to the end of the night, you can keep your job."

Before the zipper even reaches her lower back, the top of her strapless dress starts falling forward, revealing her bare tits that are small, perky handfuls with bright pink pointed nipples. Lower and lower I go down her tan body until the waistband of a pair of black lace panties are uncovered. After passing over the curve of her hips the dress sinks to the floor and pools around her ankles.

I figure she'll be yanking the material back up to cover her mostly naked body within ten seconds at most. Instead, she just stands there between my thighs unflinching. She must be in shock.

Glancing up at her perfect, flawless, completely blank face, I can't figure out what she's thinking.

"Well, what's it going to be?" I ask her.

Some of the guys at the game tables finally notice the topless woman standing at the bar and let out a few whistles and catcalls.

Naomi clears her throat and then jerks her ID that I forgot I was still holding in my right hand from between my fingers. She goes on to leave me speechless when she shoves the card down the front of her miniscule panties and asks, "Is there a certain type of whiskey you prefer, or will Jack Daniels do?"

"Jack works," I agree, unable to lift my eyes from the smooth, flat golden skin right above her narrow string waistband, looking so damn tempting that my fingers twitch wanting to touch her.

"Coming right up," she says before she slips out from between my legs and grabs up her tray. As she walks away, I get a nice long look at her jiggling ass cheeks hanging out either side of her thong before her lower body disappears behind the bar.

A moment later, Naomi brings me the entire bottle of Jack, plopping it down on the bar in front of me with a lowball glass. And then, without a word, she leaves to make the rounds on the game tables with her shoulders back and tits proudly lifted, not the least bit bothered by her nudity, or at least not showing it.

Guess the girl has more nerve than I gave her credit for.

The numbers on the pages of invoices in front of me are all but forgotten as I sit back and drink my whiskey straight from the bottle while watching her float around the room, making games halt until she disappears to fetch beers.

Despite how tempting she looks, not a single man lays a hand on her except to slip their cash into the front of her panties now and then to join her ID, perhaps because they're scared of the consequences from the Aces that are always keeping an eye out on the room along with at least four security cameras.

The night is so uneventful and even slow that I'm about to force myself to turn around and get back to work when Fiasco's palm reaches out and lands with a loud smack on Naomi's ass. He pulls her down onto his lap for a few seconds, whispers something in her ear and then lets her up.

It takes every bit of restraint in my body to keep from jumping up and going over to knock his lights out. I've always been possessive of my women, but I've never had this sort of knee-jerk reaction over a woman I've never been inside. And not once have I wanted to lay a hand on one of my own brothers because of a random girl.

I need to get a fucking grip, I know that. But it's easier said than done, especially when I start wondering if Fiasco will be taking the new girl home tonight. I don't like that thought one fucking bit. I try to tell myself that I only feel protective over Naomi because she looks so innocent and young, even strutting around in just her heels and panties.

When she comes back up to the bar counter, there's a new, rosy flush on her cheeks, like she's embarrassed or offended by Fiasco's rough treatment.

Her blue eyes meet mine and she says, "I'm fine," before I even say a word. The woman knew exactly what I was thinking with just a glance. I never let my face give away my hand, so I look back down at my papers while I force myself to relax.

This girl is going to be trouble, my head warns me. *She doesn't belong here, and she sure as shit doesn't deserve to be passed around by all of my brothers like some kind of plaything. They'll devour her and then throw her away quicker than a used rubber, snuffing out her breathtaking radiance before I can snap my fingers.*

Fuck, I'm going soft in my old age of thirty-five.

Taking a swig of whiskey from the bottle, I swallow it down and mutter under my breath, "You won't last a fucking week." I think my words are more of a hope than a prediction of her determination.

"Wanna bet?" Naomi asks confidently with a grin as she grabs two bottles of beer from our bartender and struts back over to Fiasco's table, his bright red handprint glowing on her right ass cheek, marking her as his.

Oh, fuck no.

He may have already had her, but I'll be damned if he lays another finger on her.

"*Fiasco!*" I shout before I even know what the fuck I'm doing or why. When everyone in the room stops talking to turn and look at me, I say to him, "Meeting in the chapel when we dock. Spread the word."

"Sure thing, prez," he responds with a mock salute, not having a clue how close I've come to beating his ass tonight over some girl I don't even know.

CHAPTER FIVE

Naomi

"Here you go," I say cheerfully despite the inner turmoil raging inside me when I hand Fiasco and the older man he's playing blackjack with their fresh beers.

"Thanks, babe," Fiasco says, stuffing a folded up twenty-dollar bill into the front of my panties where a few others remain since the guys have been treating me like I'm a stripper, all thanks to Malcolm fucking Hyde.

Harry was right – that guy is an asshole, which makes me feel a little less guilty about stealing from him right underneath his nose. I can't believe he had the audacity to take my dress off in the middle of the freaking room and then demand that I keep working the rest of the night in nothing but my thong. It's humiliating and demeaning, and I hate him for it. Who the hell does he think he is?

Oh, right. He's the president of the Dirty Aces; and in the blink of his intense green eyes, he could fire me. That's why I have to suck it up and do whatever he says. I thought maybe he would want the same sort of treatment as Fiasco did, but Anika was right — he turned me down flat.

Part of me was even a little disappointed by his rejection. He's apparently physically attracted to me since I sure as shit felt the hard, thick inches between his legs, so I don't get why he turned me down like all the others.

After Malcolm takes his paperwork back to his office and I have a few minutes alone with Ronnie, the bartender who trained me earlier, I lower my voice and lean on the counter to get her take on the strange man. "What's the deal with Malcolm?"

"Oh, he's harmless," she tells me with a wave of her hand. "Well, in some ways. He doesn't sleep with any of the hired staff, but one time, he did put a bullet in the man who accused him of cheating at poker."

"Seriously?" I ask in disbelief.

"Oh yeah. Trust and loyalty are big with him. Come to think of it, all of the Aces are a little trigger happy. And a bunch of man-whores, well, except for Malcolm and Nash. Just don't get too attached to any of them. I've seen the guys pull their dicks out of one girl and into another without missing a thrust."

"Ah, that's good to know," I tell her even though it's a little too late since I've already hooked up with Fiasco.

"No problem," Ronnie replies with a shrug. "At least they pay well."

"Right," I agree. Even on slow nights like tonight, the tips have been great. That could also be partly due to the fact that I'm topless and in just my panties, though.

Wiping down the counter with a rag, Ronnie goes on to say, "To be honest, I've never seen Malcolm treat anyone the way he did you tonight. I'm not sure if that's a good thing, though."

"What do you mean?"

"He's testing you, which means that he doesn't trust you. Not that Malcolm really trusts anyone but his brothers. He still makes me take a sip from opened bottles of liquor before he'll drink from it."

"Wow. The guy sounds a little paranoid."

"Who wouldn't be after what he's been through," she says.

"What has he been through?"

"You must not be from around here. Everyone knows about how the Ace of Spades MC went up in flames thanks to another biker gang, the Savage Kings, being pissed with them for doing business with the cartel."

"No, I didn't know that."

"They lost so many guys that the MC had to fold. Malcolm, Lowell and Nash were the only ones left, and they formed the Dirty Aces just two years back. That's why there are only six members right now. Well, there were seven until just recently, but Lowell betrayed them, and...well, the less said about that, the better."

"Oh. Well, ah, thanks for the history report," I tell her, glad to have any information I can get on these guys.

Time is not on my side. I need to do what I came here to do and then get the hell out before anyone figures out what I'm up to. Because if I get caught or fail, I doubt I'll ever see my twenty-second birthday.

∽

Malcolm

"What's with the late-night meeting, boss? I'm tired as fuck," Devlin says, pulling his disheveled jet-black hair back and tying it up with a rubber band.

"This couldn't wait," I tell them when we all gather around the table in the back room behind the bar. Most of the lights are out, and it's quiet in the clubhouse since it's well after two a.m.

"So, what's so important?" Nash asks with an annoyed look in his amber eyes.

"We're throwing cash out every fucking day in garbage bags," I tell them.

"Huh?" Wirth mutters around a yawn he covers with the back of his tattooed knuckles. "Do you mean that literally or what? I'm too tired to know if you're being serious or speaking metaphorically."

"What I mean is that we're wasting money on bullshit and not bringing enough in," I explain. "Dev, I want you and Fiasco to hunt down each and every person who owes us a gambling debt, no matter how big or small. If they don't have the cash to pay up, you start taking their shit – cars, flat screens, iPhones, anything we can sell to show them we mean business."

"Okay," Devlin agrees. "But is there a reason this couldn't wait until tomorrow, boss?"

"Keep your fucking panties on," I tell him, turning to Fiasco. "And you. Why the fuck did you hire another waitress for weekdays on the boat?"

"Because she's hot as hell," he replies with a smirk. "Besides, she was desperate. Also, everyone knows that hot asses bring in repeat customers who think they have a chance of hitting that."

"She's an extra expense we didn't need. And a possible liability if she tries to come at us for harassment or whatever. One look at her and you know she won't mix with our customers. The girl looks like a goddamn high school virgin!"

"Sounds like I need to see this girl for myself," Silas grins, making me glare at him.

"She could be a narc or a gold-digger looking for her next jackpot by threatening assault charges on us."

"Naomi wouldn't do nothin' like that, man," Fiasco says. "Even if she did try to bring up charges, I'm in the clear since I've got her on video consenting before she put my dick in her mouth."

"I fucking knew it!" I exclaim as I slam my palms down on the table. "You and your dick are gonna be the death of us all!"

"It's just a blowie, boss," Dev says. "I've gotten at least one from every other waitress who's ever worked for us."

"Not anymore," I tell them.

"Huh?" Wirth asks again, apparently the only word he's capable of in the middle of the night.

"I'm putting my foot down. You all need to keep it in your fucking pants on the job, whether it's here in the bar, on the boat, or at the chop shop."

"Ain't no chicks working at the chop shop," Fiasco points out.

"You're not that picky about where you put your dick," I challenge. "I doubt if Drake or Hudson's ass is completely out of the question."

"Whoa. That's a low blow, prez, even for you," Silas mutters.

"Look, all I'm saying is that if we want our businesses to keep growing so we can bring in new members and expand to more charters, we need to be more careful with our spending and not make any stupid decisions."

"Yeah, okay," Devlin agrees.

"Whatever," Wirth grumbles.

"Fine by me," Nash says. "I don't want any part of the disease-ridden girls who are desperate enough to fuck this bunch of assholes."

"So, does that mean you've been eyeing Drake or Hudson's ass?" Devlin teases Nash, who flips him both of his middle fingers.

"Fuck you and your pharmacy of STD antibiotics, Dev."

"Silas, Fiasco, do we have your word that you'll keep your dicks out of staff and your heads in the game?"

"You're taking away our easy pussy, man," Silas argues. "But fine, what the hell. I can get some ass wherever I want it."

"Fiasco?" I say.

"Can I still fuck them if they're not on the clock?" he asks.

"Think of all the cash you'll be saving if you avoid the additional child support, buddy," Devlin says to Fiasco, who has at least two baby mamas that we know of.

"Yeah. Okay," he huffs. "Still, it's fucked up you give us this new rule right after Naomi's fine ass comes along."

"You'll live," I assure him. Now I just have to convince myself that tonight's late meeting and my decision isn't just about the new girl.

CHAPTER SIX

Naomi

The drunk customers on the cruise are such easy targets. So far none have noticed when I slide their cell phones out of their pockets or 'borrow' their wallets before returning them with credit card numbers written down. They blame the alcohol on losing their shit, and I've been making a killing.

Thanks to my tips, along with the stolen goods and extra cash I've been able to siphon off of alcohol sales, I've made almost five thousand dollars in just one week working for the Aces. That means I'm getting closer to paying off the twenty thousand I owe Harry; and at the moment, I would literally do anything to get him off my back with his outrageous interest rates.

Oddly enough, Fiasco hasn't touched me since the night Malcolm made me strip down to serve drinks, even though the blond man still looks at me like he's thinking dirty thoughts. Actually, I've come to realize that's pretty much Fiasco's expression whenever he looks at any woman.

And Malcolm? Well, each day he watches me a little longer, a little more closely, making it increasingly more difficult to slip a few extra dollars into my cleavage. Difficult, but not impossible.

"Guess what," I say when I waltz up to the man in charge on my eighth night.

"What?" he asks, avoiding eye contact with me and preferring to study the room.

"It's been over a week and I still haven't quit," I remark.

"You want me to throw you a party?"

"No," I reply. "A simple *congratulations, I was wrong* will do."

"In your fucking dreams, honey," he says with a soft chuckle as he pulls out a cigarette and lights it up.

"Speaking of dreams," I start, leaning my hip against the stool next to his. "What do you dream about, Malcolm? Or should I say whom?"

An arched eyebrow as he sucks on his cancer stick is his silent response, but at least now he's looking right at me.

"Men or women?" I ask softly, causing him to cough when he starts choking on his smoke.

Ronnie eyes both of us curiously from behind the bar before she fills a glass with water and sets it on the bar for Malcolm. He quickly picks it up and guzzles it down. Once he's finished the water off, he slams the glass on the bar and wipes his mouth with the back of his hand. "The fuck did you just ask me?"

"You heard me," I say. Ronnie is standing too close now for me to repeat it without definitely pissing him off, if I haven't already.

"Screw it," Malcolm says, glancing away from me. "I'll leave that one up to your imagination, honey."

I take a step closer to his thigh before I quietly say next to his ear, "Then I choose you and Fiasco...together. The question is...who would be the top?"

Quicker than a snake, Malcolm strikes, grabbing a handful of my hair and tugging on it hard when he pulls my head down to speak into my ear. "I don't know what you're playing at, little girl, but that mouth of yours is going to land you in a world of hurt if you don't watch it."

"Guess that answers my question," I reply breathlessly.

"I should've fired you the first night," Malcolm says as he pulls my hair tighter so that my face is only inches from his.

"Why didn't you?" I ask.

"Hell if I know. Keep running your mouth and I'll have to rethink my decision. Now get the fuck back to work."

"Yes, sir," I reply as he releases his hold on me. "Can I get you anything? Maybe a fifth of whiskey?"

"Jack Daniels," he responds and starts to turn away before he adds, "And if Jack were still alive, he'd be the only one I'd ever consider fucking. You can bet your ass he'd be a bottom too."

Despite all of his threats and attempts to scare me, I can't help myself when a smile spreads across my face.

"Watch out, Jack," I mutter before I reach over the bar to grab a bottle of the amber liquid, intentionally letting my skirt rise up the back of my thighs because I know Malcolm is looking.

∼

Malcolm

NAOMI's fine ass is within slapping distance, begging for a palm to claim it as she reaches over the bar.

I know exactly what she's doing, but it won't work.

No matter how badly I want to fuck the mouthy blonde's brains out, I won't do it. I swear she's been sent to earth to test me, to tempt me, because I've never had as much trouble keeping my dick down as I do around her. The damn thing has a mind of its own, standing up proud and ready to report for duty when I didn't request his services.

Maybe Silas was right, I need to get off before I go fucking insane and kill someone. Each day that I abstain I get a little crankier, a little less stable and a helluva lot hornier. And there's nothing stopping me from calling up one of my usual girls and taking care of business except for one smart-mouthed, too sexy for her own good, waitress. Without even trying, I know that Naomi's face and ass and tits are the ones I'll see when I'm inside any other woman. It'll be her mouth wrapped around my dick, her mouth begging me for more. I may be an asshole of the highest order, but even I wouldn't use another woman just to pretend she's someone else.

This is not a problem I've ever had before. Women are women. They all have asses and tits and pussies that feel equally amazing. I've never even been all that picky, willing to screw the curviest girl in the room or the thinnest, the shortest or tallest. I don't even care all that much about their faces as long as their bodies put in the work.

Until now.

The only reason I haven't pulled Naomi on my lap and fucked her in front of everyone on the boat yet is because I know Fiasco's been keeping his hands off of her.

Why am I so sure about that?

Because I'm barely able to let her out of my sight while she's on the clock unless duty calls, and then, after hours, I've followed her home after we dock like some sort of creepy stalker.

She's becoming an unhealthy obsession; one I can't seem to shake.

And the worst part?

My gut says there's something...off about her. Why would someone like her choose to be here, working on a dangerous boat with outlaws? It doesn't make sense. I've ran a background check on her and even followed her home three different times to see if she has any ties to rival groups, or even worse, law enforcement.

So far? Nothing.

MALCOLM

Every night after the boat docks, Naomi goes straight home to a white, two-story farmhouse, alone. Why am I so sure she lives there alone? There are no other cars in the driveway; and as soon as she walks inside, she flips on each and every light as she goes through the place and leaves them on, like she's scared of the dark.

I've become so fixated on her that I even manhandled her right in the middle of the casino with everyone watching when she ran her mouth.

She was messing with me, trying to rile me up. And it fucking worked.

No one has ever had that kind of effect on my cool and calm demeanor. It's...unsettling. Naomi unsettles the fuck out of me.

I need to put more distance between us and fast before this shit gets worse and I do something crazy like take her home with me, tie her to my bed, and pound inside of her body until I finally get my fill of her. Even if that takes hours or days...

"Fuck," I mutter aloud, causing Naomi to startle as she was pouring my Jack into a glass.

"You okay?" she asks with her brow furrowing.

"Just give me the bottle so I can get back to work," I snap at her, not because she's done anything wrong other than not being restrained to my bed twenty-four seven like I want.

"Here you go," she says as she hands over the bottle.

"Thanks," I huff as I take a long swig and carry it in a death grip back to my office.

CHAPTER SEVEN

Malcolm

It's been two weeks since Naomi started working on the boat, which is a week longer than I predicted. I'm not usually wrong about these things. My intuition is always dead-on, so what the fuck am I missing with this girl?

Lately, I've made myself stop gawking at her from the bar, which just means that now I do it from my office with my feet up on my desk, smoking a cigarette and watching her on the surveillance camera app on my phone when I should be working on the books. I've convinced myself that I'm keeping an eye on her for the good of the MC when really I just can't seem to take my eyes off of her for more than a few seconds, worried one of the guys will try and feel her up; and if so, I'll have to break their hands.

And it's a damn good thing I'm keeping a close eye on Naomi too, or I may have missed the sleight of hand when someone orders a drink and she stuffs the cash down the front of her tight black dress.

At first, I don't think anything of it. But then I zoom in on her and watch her do it over and over again instead of putting the money in the register at the bar.

I try and convince myself that at the end of the night, she'll settle up for the drinks, but she doesn't when we dock. She simply leaves...

"I fucking knew it!" I say aloud as I jump to my feet.

And goddamn, I really hate that I was right about her. I wanted her to be different, even though I have no clue why.

I'm so fucking enraged by her betrayal that I want to break something. The closest thing in my reach is my desk; so, with one sweep of my arm, I send everything on it flying. Ashtrays, paperwork, a money drawer, all of it ends up hitting the opposite wall and crashing to the floor.

Once everything is wiped clear, I hunch over the desk feeling absolutely defeated, my palms spread and head hanging so low the ends of my long hair nearly brush the desktop.

Nothing feels worse than betrayal. It's nearly impossible to trust anyone nowadays, which is why I don't usually fall for anyone's bullshit.

This time, with Naomi though, I did. I fell for her sweet, innocent act and thought she really was here to work and earn money. Instead, she's stealing mine and the MC's cash right out of our pockets.

Since I know from experience that I need hardcore evidence before I start accusing someone of theft, I grab my phone to shoot a text message to Ronnie, asking her to come to my office before she leaves for the night.

"Yes, sir?" she asks a moment later when she peeks through the cracked door, sounding out of breath from getting here in a hurry. Her eyes widen when she takes in the mess on my floor.

"Come in and shut the door," I tell her.

She slips inside and does as I asked, clutching her hands behind her back.

"I need you to do inventory tonight. I know it's short notice, but I'll pay you double for the overtime, if that's okay?"

"Sure, yeah."

"Tomorrow night too. And not just cases, I want every single bottle accounted for. Do you understand?"

"Yes, sir."

"Good. And Ronnie?"

"Yes?"

"Don't tell anyone about what I'm asking you to do."

"Is there a problem..." she trails off.

"You just go do your job and report back to me each night. Got it?"

"Yes, sir."

CHAPTER EIGHT

Naomi

I think Malcolm's avoiding me.

I've barely seen him the past week when before he was always around with his eyes on me.

I don't like how not having his constant attention makes me feel so unnerved and unsettled. It shouldn't matter. I should be glad that I have a little more freedom, not thinking the worst.

It's probably just the guilt talking. I've banked almost ten thousand dollars, not that I get to keep even a penny of that. All of it has been dropped into the bank and wired to Harry, who needs more money like he needs another twelve dozen doughnuts.

"Malcolm wants to see you in his office," Ronnie informs me when I go to the bar to pick up another round of beers for a group of guys playing poker.

"Okay. I'll stop by his office after I drop off these beers."

"No. Go now," she whispers without looking at me. "Why aren't you walking yet? Go!"

"Now?" I ask again in confusion as my palms turn sweaty with an onslaught of nervousness. Malcolm's never invited me into his office before. Is that a good thing or a bad thing? And why when I think of good do I automatically think of him unzipping my dress again?

"Now, Naomi. I'll take this round to the poker table," Ronnie assures me.

"All right. Thanks," I say as I turn and make my way down the hallway to Malcolm's office. I rap my knuckles on the closed door, and a moment later his deep voice calls back, "Come in."

My heart is about to thump out of my chest when I step inside.

"Shut the door," Malcolm orders from where he's sitting behind a big wooden desk. His boots are propped up on it, crossed casually at the ankle while a cloud of smoke billows up from the cigarette resting between two of his fingers.

At least he looks cool and calm, not angry.

"You wanted to see me?" I ask when we're shut inside the room alone together.

His intense eyes stare at me, unblinking for so long that I nearly breakdown then and there, spilling all of my secrets.

Oh shit.

He *is* angry. Like, about to snap someone's bones angry about something, and I think that something could be me. I feel more naked now standing before him in my dress than I did the night he stripped me down to my panties.

"Come here," he growls into the silence, startling me with the harsh intensity of the words.

Uh-oh.

Swallowing down a bad case of the nerves, I slowly make my way over until I'm standing beside his desk near his feet. A second later, he pounces on me, so fast I didn't even see him stand up. I just blink, and then he's towering over me, his immense size making me gasp. He's always intimidating when he's just sitting down at the bar, but now he's just plain scary standing at least a foot taller than me with his linebacker shoulders blocking out the rest of the room. He's so close I have to tilt my head backward to see his face. Malcolm takes a drag off his cigarette and blows the smoke out of the corner of his lips before reaching around me to put it out in the ashtray, which means the front of his body is pressed even tighter to mine. From the corner of my eye, I then see him reach down and pull something from his pocket or his belt, but I don't know what it is until the sharp point of what can only be a knife is pressing into the center of my chest.

A yelp of surprise escapes me before I find my voice again. "Wh-what are you doing?" I ask him.

He lowers the point until it meets the top of my dress. Grabbing the material with his free hand, the other slices the blade through the fabric, cutting my dress straight down the middle with enough force that I feel the pressure, but it doesn't leave a mark on my skin. All the tips I've stuffed inside earlier float down to the floor around our feet, causing Malcolm to growl angrily through his gritted teeth.

"Those are-are my tips," I tell him as I slap my palms over my bare breasts, feeling way too exposed at the moment wearing only a pair of red panties.

"Sure they are," is his stony reply. "No need to act shy now and cover yourself up. Wasn't it just a few weeks ago that you were rubbing your pussy on my dick like you wanted to ride it?"

"Y-yes," I answer, remembering the embarrassing moment when he said he would never fuck me.

"So, what's the matter? You changed your mind?"

"No." I shake my head to confirm my answer. "No, sir." Malcolm may be scary at the moment, but I still want him. I've wanted him since the second I saw him, even though I know I shouldn't.

"We'll see about that."

Closing the knife on the edge of his desk beside my thigh, he thankfully slips it back into his belt holster. As soon as his hands are free, though, he spins me around and presses his large palm between my shoulder blades, roughly forcing my bare upper body down until the side of my face is flat against a stack of papers on his desk.

"There's nothing I hate more than liars except for *thieves*," he mutters. Crap. He knows! "Do you have any idea how furious I am with you?" Keeping one strong hand on the center of my back, the other comes up over my hip, giving my panties a tug when he starts to peel them down my legs.

I shake my head no as much as I can because I'm incapable of speaking now that he has me naked and bent over the desk like he's not planning on letting me up anytime soon. I don't know if he's going to whip me or kill me or fuck me for stealing from him.

He said a few weeks ago that he would never fuck me; but he put the knife away, so I think I can probably cross *kill me* off the list. Maybe. Hopefully.

"Wh-what are you going to do to me?" I cave and ask.

Placing his lips against my ear, his teeth nip at the cuff before he whispers, "I'm going to fucking ruin you."

Those six threatening words are still echoing in my head when Malcolm runs one of his thick fingertips crudely down the crease of my ass, over my puckered hole, heading lower...

"Are you hiding *my* money anywhere else?" he asks.

"N-*nooo*," I cry out when he suddenly shoves his finger right up inside of my pussy none too gently. Not that he was met with any resistance. It's impossible not to notice how wet I am or the ease at which he slides his finger in and out, in and out, before adding another, making me gasp.

"D-don't stop," I beg although I know I'm in deep trouble. The only good sign is that he's leaning more toward fucking my brains out than murdering me at the moment.

Malcolm called me a thief. He knows I've stolen from him. But at this very moment, I can't find it in me to care that he's so angry he's obviously snapped, losing a grip on whatever restraint kept him from touching me for the last few weeks no matter how much I flirted with him. From this position, I have no choice but to take whatever punishment he has in store for me, and I want it all, everything he wouldn't give to the other women who tried to tempt him and failed.

Ruin me, that's what he's promised to do.

Although, as the familiar liquid warmth starts to gather and intensify in my lower belly, I'm starting to think that what Malcolm is planning to do to me is going to be more of a reward than a punishment.

∽

Malcolm

I'VE BEEN FUCKING furious ever since I saw the surveillance video of Naomi stealing from the club.

Ronnie brought me proof not one, not two, but three damn nights in a row. During that time, I had to just sit back and watch Naomi steal not only from the MC over and over again, but from our motherfucking customers!

When I finally called her in to my office tonight, I wanted to scare her, to make her tell me why she took what wasn't hers and to make her pay. That's why I pulled out my knife and sliced up her dress. I thought she would be terrified, that she would break down crying and beg me to not hurt her.

Instead, in some bizarre twist of events I orchestrated without thinking them through, she's bent over my desk naked and moaning with her ass squirming in the air, looking like a fucking fantasy come true. Despite my rough handling, or maybe because of it, her pussy is so wet for me that her juices are coating the inside of her thighs while I keep fucking her with my fingers.

I thought she would've screamed for me to stop as soon as I slid my fingers through her folds, but she didn't. In fact, her only words were, *"Don't stop."*

Now my dick is so swollen behind the zipper of my jeans that it may burst. And right this second, there's only one place I want to put it. No, there's only one place I *need* to put it to ease the constant ache I've had only for her going on more than two fucking weeks.

It makes no sense at all why I would want to fuck the thief, but I do. I've never slept with any of our hired girls before because it's bad for business. That's why I made the guys lay off of them, not so Fiasco would have to keep his hands off of Naomi. At least not just for that reason...

This, tonight, isn't just about finally sating an urge with Naomi. It's also about punishing her, taking out my anger on her sexy little tease of a body, not just for stealing from us but for making me go so fucking insane I can't think straight anymore. All I do every minute of the day is imagine dragging her back here to my office and getting her underneath me so no other man can have her but me. It's an irrational thought that needs to stop, and it will after tonight when I finally take what I want from her and then send her on her way to drive some other man insane while she steals from him.

Unable to stop myself after going this far, I keep pumping my fingers in and out of Naomi's tight cunt and use my free hand to unzip my jeans. Pulling out my hard shaft, I stroke it a few rough times before I withdraw my fingers and replace them with the fat head of my cock. Her pussy is so hot and slick I ease right on inside. Naomi gasps and moans underneath me as I fill her with one slow, agonizing inch at a time until I meet resistance. I'm as deep as I can physically go and still it's not enough. Her pussy is heaven and hell all wrapped into one. Tight and perfect. It's too incredible to ever leave while at the same time it's torturous knowing I shouldn't be here in paradise in the first place.

"Fuck," I groan as I still my hips and curl my fingers around the back of her neck. "Should've known you'd feel too damn good to be a one-off. You're not a cock-tease. You're a fucking cock-vortex, sucking men inside and never letting them go."

I give her a few seconds to adjust before I plan to fuck her brains out. And honestly, I need a moment myself because I've never done this before, gone into a woman's cunt bare without protection. It's idiotic and dangerous, but it's too late now that I've felt her silky flesh that fits me so damn nice and snug, like a glove that's two sizes too small. One I can't wait to stretch the fuck out.

"Move, Malcolm!" Naomi pleads as her fingers curl tightly around the opposite edge of my desk. The desperation in her voice almost makes me do as she asked. *Almost.* I want to give her exactly what she's demanding, but on my own time. It would serve her right if I didn't let her come at all, just use her body to get myself off and then send her home with an aching need she'll never forget.

Hauling back my palm, I slap the shit out of the meaty part of her ass, making it bounce off the desk thanks to the pain or the surprise. I hope it was both. I want the shape of my palm to mark her, just like Fiasco did a few weeks ago. Then, hating the reminder that she put her sexy lips around his dick, I smack her ass again and again before I remind her, "You don't get to give the orders. I'm the one in charge here!"

The truth is, I'm dying to pull out and slam back inside as hard as possible. Instead of giving in to that need to punish her, I just swivel my hips in a circle.

"Oh god, yes!" she shouts at the movement, squirming her ass around on the desk to try and get the friction she needs.

Grabbing a handful of the back of Naomi's hair, I give a tug, and when she looks over her shoulder at me, I warn her, "I'm gonna fuck you so hard you'll feel me for days. And then you're going to tell me why the hell *you* have been fucking *me*."

While her eyes are still on mine, I pull back and then thrust into her so deep and fast the desk moves under us, making her gasp sharply. "And if you lie to me again, you'll regret it. Do you understand me?" I ask.

"Yes," she whispers.

I make her chant that same word over and over as I slam inside of her again and again until her entire body trembles from head to toe. When her inner walls start to pulse around my intruding thickness, it's like nothing I've ever experienced before. At this very second, I want nothing more than to burn every condom in the world for making me miss out on this sensation until now.

My release comes out of nowhere, hitting me like a bolt of lightning down my spine as I quickly pull out of her cunt and stroke myself, once, twice. Ropes of cum erupt all over Naomi's sweet ass cheeks before it starts running down her inner thighs, onto my desk. I love seeing my seed on her skin, soaking it up, so much so that another pleasurable tremor throws me so off balance I have to slam my palm down on the desk to hold myself up.

As soon as I'm able to stand up and take a step back from Naomi, she slowly sinks down to the floor like her limbs aren't capable of holding her up any longer.

I walk around the back of my desk to grab some tissues to clean up my dick and by the time I turn around, she's sitting in the pile of dollar bills with her back to the wooden desk, head thrown back, plump lips parted and still panting. Her short, blonde hair is damp around the front of her rosy face, the evidence of how much she enjoyed our romp that never should've happened.

Since it's too late to do anything about my stupid decision, it's time I finally get some answers out of her before I throw her ass off my boat.

Well, once we get back to the dock. I'm not a completely ruthless asshole.

After zipping up my pants, I drag my rolling chair around to park it in front of where she's sitting. Grabbing my lighter and pack of Marlboros from the top of the desk, I drop down into the seat with my legs spread wide so I can still see her face.

"So, how long have you been stealing from me? Since day one?" I ask as I stick the smoke in my mouth and light it up.

"Could I...could I maybe put some clothes on first?" she asks, reaching for her discarded and ripped dress on the floor. My boot gets there first. I stomp on the black fabric and slide it over to my chair so I can snatch it up in my fist to keep it from her.

"No clothes until you answer all of my fucking questions," I inform her. Besides, it's no hardship to talk to her with her tits out. Or they were visible before she lets out a heavy sigh and pulls her knees up to her chest, wrapping her arms around them, blocking all but a peek of her cunt from view. "How long have you been skimming cash from my drinks and stealing from my customers, Naomi?" I ask again.

"Since...I started working on the boat," she tells me without even a hint of remorse on her face or in her voice.

"Why?"

"Because...because I had to."

"Try again," I say.

Her big, blue eyes stare up at me pleadingly. "I swear I didn't want to, Malcolm. But I didn't have a choice!"

"Bullshit. There's always a choice," I counter, unaffected by her acting like the innocent victim. That shit doesn't fly when she's sitting naked on the floor of my office after I was inside of her, the smell of our combined bodily fluids still lingering in the air so thick I can almost taste the sex on my tongue.

"There wasn't a choice in my case," she mutters while tightening her arms around her knees.

"Come on, honey. Just spit it out already! Now you're just wasting my time, which is only going to piss me off even more," I say, getting annoyed now thanks to the way my dick overtakes my common sense where this girl is concerned. That shit has *never* happened to me before. There have been plenty of women I wanted to fuck but didn't because I knew they were either not worth the hassle, off-limits, or trouble waiting to happen.

Naomi shakes her head in refusal. "I can't tell you."

"Yes, you can, and you will. All you have to do is open your pretty little mouth, you know, like you did to convince Fiasco to give you this job. Just use your words now instead of your gag reflex."

"No, really. I *can't*," she replies.

I reach above her head to flick the end of my smoke into the ashtray, crowding her when I say, "Then you're not leaving this room or getting clothes again until you change your mind."

Her eyes widen as they lock with mine, like she's trying to judge my sincerity. I'm as serious as a fucking heart attack. We're both gonna sit right here until she talks.

When her shoulders sag and her gaze drops, I know she's realized the truth for herself, that I'm not going to budge and that she's screwed. I've got her right where I want her, leaving her no choice. Of course she can try to lie her way out of this, but I don't think she's stupid enough to try and bullshit me again.

"You're going to kill me when you find out," she says simply, not as though she's being facetious, but like she actually believes I'm not only a murderer but that I would be willing to kill a woman I just fucked. Sure, anything is possible, but I doubt there's anything she can say to make me homicidal right now with my cock well sated.

"Sooner or later I'm going to find out, so you may as well tell me before I torture it out of you," I tell her.

The rosy glow on her face instantly whitens after my threat, likely imagining the worst. If she could see inside my head, she would know that I'm picturing torturing her by fucking her cunt with my tongue and not letting her come until she's ready to talk.

Clearing her throat, she says, "Do you...do you know Harold Cox?"

"*Harry* Cox? Hell yeah, I know that fat, aptly named bastard. Why? Wait. Are you fucking him?" I ask in disbelief.

"Ew, god no," she answers with a shiver that I believe is genuine. "I...borrowed something from him..."

"You stole from him."

"Yes, fine. I stole something; and when he found out, he wasn't happy," she admits.

"I'm familiar with the concept," I mutter. "How much was this... something worth?"

"Twenty-thousand. But with interest I now owe him, twenty-five thousand or a little more."

I let loose a whistle because that's a big chunk of cash, one he would probably require her to pay back with twenty-five percent interest or more, constantly growing and growing.

"So you were stealing from me to pay him back?" I ask.

"Sort of."

"Explain," I snap at her.

"I guess he doesn't like you or the MC, maybe both," Naomi tells me with a shrug of her narrow shoulders.

Taking one last drag from my cigarette, I blow the smoke out of my nose and then lean forward to put it out in the ashtray on the desk before I respond. "Me. Harry doesn't like me."

"Oh," she mutters. "Well, anyway, I told him I didn't have his money, so he gave me two options..."

"And they were?"

Squeezing her eyes shut, she says, "The first was that he would sell me to the highest bidder among all his rich friends to make back the twenty thousand I took."

"Sell you?" I repeat. "Like hand you over to be someone's sex slave?"

"Yep," she answers. "Or *rent* me out to them." When she looks back up at me, I can see the fear of that happening to her in her blue eyes and know that she's telling the truth.

"And the second option?" I ask.

"He said I could steal the money from you. He told me that you would be..."

"Be what?" I prod when she pauses.

Naomi rests her chin on top of her knees and holds my gaze. "An easy target."

"Easy?" I scoff. "He fucking said that I would be an *easy* target?"

"Yes."

"Wow. That fucker is even dumber than I thought," I say while shaking my head at his fucking audacity.

"Whether he's stupid or not doesn't matter. I'm screwed; because if you don't kill me, he's probably going to sell me."

"I'm not going to kill you," I assure her. "And I knew from day one that you didn't belong here. All you had to do to get Fiasco to hire you was blow him?"

"Yes."

Groaning up at the ceiling, I mutter, "That dick of his is going to be the death of him one of these days."

"Right, well, um, can I have some clothes so I can leave now?" she asks.

"No."

"No? You said..."

"That I wouldn't kill you," I reiterate. "You think I'm going to let you get up and leave now that I know Harry-fucking-Cox sent you to *steal* from me? Sorry, honey, but that's not going to happen."

"What? But...I can't just sit around here! Harry *will* send someone for me if I don't get him the rest of the money I owe him by the end of next week! I don't want to be a sex slave for dirty old men!"

"How much more do you owe him?" I ask.

"A little over ten grand."

"Nah, you don't need ten thousand dollars."

"Ah, yes I do!"

"No, you don't," I assure her. "You sure do like to argue, don't you?"

"Without the money, I'm screwed."

"You're right. If you don't pay what you owe Harry, he probably will do what he threatened. He's apparently not very forgiving."

"Why doesn't he like you?" she asks.

"I stole a gold-digging bitch from him just because I could and then gave her the boot," I tell her honestly. "Guess he still hasn't gotten over her preferring me to him."

"You or him? That's not really a choice..."

Arching my eyebrow at her, I say, "Guess I'll take that as a compliment. But fuck Harry and his woman. What the hell am I going to do with you?"

CHAPTER NINE

Naomi

I'm sitting on the floor naked in Malcolm's office, completely at his mercy as he contemplates what he's going to do to me for catching me stealing from him. I feel a wave of déjà vu that's quickly overwhelmed with a twisting despair in my stomach.

"Is this going to be a multiple-choice situation too?" I ask him to try and lighten the mood.

"You think you deserve that? For me to give you choices?" Malcolm huffs as he runs his fingers through the long waves of his hair and leans back in his chair to watch me.

"I don't deserve them, no, but I still hope you'll give them to me, maybe because you feel sorry for me..."

"Why should I feel sorry for a lying thief like you?" he huffs.

"Because...because Harry is my...he's my father."

Malcolm doesn't say a word for several long seconds while I hold my breath.

"You don't have the same last name," he points out suspiciously through narrowed eyes.

"He never married my mother," I explain. "He says she was just his whore for a few years before he kicked her to the curb. I barely saw him over the years, but I needed money recently, so I paid him a visit and... stole one of his prized possessions."

"That was stupid. There are cameras everywhere now," Malcolm remarks.

"Yeah, but by the time he noticed, it was gone. I'd sold it, the money had been used, and he couldn't get it back."

"So, Harry is your biological father and he threatened to sell you, just like that?" he asks with a snap of his fingers.

"Yes. Why, are you surprised?"

"No, I guess not," he mutters.

"So, now that you know all of that, will you please work with me on how I can make things right?" I ask.

"Okay, I'll give you...three choices," Malcolm says, leaning forward with his elbows on his knees to put his face closer to mine. For a moment, I get distracted by the golden ring surrounding the green of his irises before I remember that what we're talking about is serious.

"Three choices. Great. What are they?" I ask.

"The first one is – I take you back to Harry and let him do whatever he wants with you."

"Next," I say since that's a big hell no.

"Second, you pay me back everything you owe me, which, if I understood correctly, would be fifteen-grand since you still owe him ten of the twenty-five thousand."

"That's probably an accurate accounting," I admit. "But I don't have the money. If I did, I wouldn't be stealing it from you to pay him!"

"Then you could pay me back at fifteen percent interest per month."

"No, that'll take forever," I huff. Harry's doing the same thing, continuing to add interest so that I'll never get caught up. "I want this done and over with."

Malcolm leans back in his chair and grips the arm rests. "So, I guess that leaves you with one last option."

"And what's that?"

"You start paying me back immediately with what you *do* happen to have available..."

"I don't have *anything* of monetary value available," I remind him, at least nothing I'm willing to sell.

"Sure you do," he says, tilting his head to the side and letting his eyes roam over my naked flesh. "You could pay me back with your sexy little body."

"I'm not a whore!" I exclaim indignantly.

"Didn't say you were," he replies. "In fact, it would sort of be the reverse. I'm letting *you* fuck *me* for fifteen thousand more dollars plus interest, for a total of twenty-five thousand, so that would make me a rather expensive whore."

"No. Absolutely not," I tell him adamantly.

"Then, I guess you'll have to take your chances with your father's rich friends and their saggy balls, hairy backs, and bellies so big you have to lift the fat up to get to their shriveled cocks..."

"Fine!" I exclaim after he paints that disgusting picture. "At least you're sort of nice to look at," I add, making him smirk because we both know I'm full of shit. Malcolm Hyde is hot as fuck, and he definitely knows how to use the dangerous weapon between his legs. "How would this really work?" I ask him.

"I would take care of what you owe Harry and the MC, which means you would owe me twenty-five thousand in total too."

"And what exactly would I have to do to earn that twenty-five thousand?" I ask.

"All you need to worry about is taking care of me and my needs," he responds. "So, what do you say? You going to work your debt off on my dick?"

That's an offensive and incredibly crude thing for a man to say to a woman. And if he hadn't just made me come on his fingers and cock, I wouldn't think twice about turning him down. But Malcolm is yummy and very talented with his body parts...

"I'll give you...one night."

"One night!" he barks out with a laugh. "Honey, you stole from me and the Dirty Aces. Do you know what happened to the last person who stole from us?"

"No," I answer.

"He's six fucking feet under!" Getting to his feet, Malcolm stands right in front of me and reaches down to tilt my chin up with his one finger. "Too bad he wasn't nearly as pretty as you are. So, the way I see it, honey, if you *were* a whore, twenty-five thousand dollars at five hundred a pop is equal to at least fifty fucks."

"Again, I'm not a whore!" I yell at him. His single finger on my chin is strong enough to snap my jaw closed.

"Hey, it's not my fault that you owe daddy money and decided to steal from me. So now you have to pay up with what you do have that can be made readily available to me– your pussy, your mouth, and your ass. All three whenever I want for fifty dirty days and fifty naughty nights."

"No," I say, turning my head so he is finally forced to let go of my chin. There's no way I'm going to be his sex toy for fifty days *and* nights! "The most I could do is...one week," I counter.

"Not even I can fuck fifty times in one week. At least I don't think so," he says when he retakes his seat. "I've never actually counted. But fine, I'm willing to compromise. Let's make it two weeks. That's my last and final offer. Take it or leave it and go spend the rest of your life sucking an old man's limp dick."

Dammit, he knows I'm stuck here with no wiggle room. And it's not like fourteen days of sex with a hot, tattooed biker is really a chore. It's much easier than being sold into sex slavery.

"Just think about how pissed daddy will be when he finds out the man he loathes is fucking his little girl..." Malcolm throws out there, sealing the deal. I hate Harry and would love to hurt him back any way possible for all the years he spent ignoring me, pretending I don't exist except as a consequence of a bad affair from long ago.

"Fine. I guess I can handle two weeks," I agree with a heavy sigh.

"You guess?" he huffs. "Honey, I just had you screaming and begging me to fuck you like a bitch in heat. You loved every second of it."

"It wasn't all bad," I say, my face burning up with shame because he's right.

He arches his eyebrow at my 'not all bad' comment but doesn't respond to it.

"Two weeks and your body is mine to do whatever I want with it, twenty-four hours a day. Agreed?"

"Agreed," I say as I swallow down that jagged pill of infinite possibilities. Who knows how rough and kinky Malcolm can get in the sack?

I can't wait to find out should not be the first thought that pops up in my head.

Malcolm offers me his palm to shake, which I take.

"Oh, and you're going to keep working for me here for free until our deal ends too," Malcolm adds while still clutching my hand. "But if I catch you stealing even one penny that isn't yours, I'll make your father look like a goddamn saint when I chain you up below deck and let every asshole who walks onto the boat have a turn with you. Do you understand me, Naomi?"

I give a nod and swallow around the new lump in my throat. I believe he would do it. He may have assured me that he wouldn't kill me; but if I cross him again, I have no doubt he'll make me pay. Malcolm doesn't seem like the forgiving type.

"Yes, sir. I won't make that mistake again," I assure him.

"Good. Now, go wash my cum from between your legs and ass cheeks and get the fuck back to work. I'll give you a ride back to my place when we dock."

"What about my clothes?" I ask as he helps pull me up to my feet. Once I'm standing, he grabs my torn black dress from the floor and ties it tightly in a tight knot around my chest, covering my breasts and part of my stomach; then kneels to help me slip my red panties back on.

"That'll work for tonight," he tells me as he gets back to his feet.

"What? I'm practically naked!" I say as I glance down at the ridiculous lack of coverage.

Malcolm whips out his big knife from his pocket and holds it up between us. "I'll rip your panties and what's left of your dress to shreds too if you don't shut the hell up and get out of my office right fucking now."

So we're right back to where we started my first night, him insisting on trying to make me uncomfortable. Well, fuck him.

"Fine. I bet my tips will be through the roof again. And by the way, I'm keeping those for myself."

"Fine," he agrees, as if I was asking his approval.

CHAPTER TEN

Malcolm

As soon as Naomi leaves my office, Fiasco is busting in, face scarlet red and eyes blazing with anger before I even get my chair pushed back behind my desk where it belongs.

"What happened to Naomi's dress?" he asks, his nostrils flaring as he sniffs the air. "And why does it smell like a bucket full of jizz in here?"

"Because I fucked her," I tell him, taking a seat and propping my feet up on the corner.

"Are you shitting me?" he exclaims. When I don't respond, he says, "I'm calling a goddamn meeting!"

"We need at least four members present for a meeting," I remind him.

"Good thing Silas and Devlin are onboard playing poker," he huffs before he turns to go get them.

Great. He's bound and determined to ruin my after-sex buzz.

And yeah, I probably should've thought about the consequences that screwing Naomi would have on Fiasco and the fact that I broke my own rule, but I didn't. All rational thoughts went out the window, pushed aside by the need to be inside of her. After nailing her once, I thought that need would start to subside.

It hasn't. Before she left my office, I was already getting hard again for her. Good thing we have the rest of the night and thirteen more days and nights to go.

A few minutes later, an annoyed Dev and Silas are filing into my office with Fiasco bringing up the rear, slamming the door behind them.

"What's up, boss?" Dev asks.

"I didn't call this meeting; Fiasco did," I tell them, propping my hands casually behind my head to wait him out. I'm feeling too fucking good to even care if he's pissed. Silas was right. I *really* needed to get laid.

"Fiasco? What the fuck?" Silas snaps at him. "I was on a winning streak!"

"He's fucking the waitress I hired!" Fiasco shouts, sounding like a two-year-old throwing a tantrum.

"Who fucked who?" Dev asks.

"Malcolm fucked Naomi! The asshole told us not to fuck the help, and then he goes and fucks her!"

"Dude, why did you fuck her?" Silas asks me.

"Because she and I have an agreement — she's going to be my sex slave for the next two weeks," I answer truthfully, causing Fiasco's pale blue eyes to nearly bulge out of his head.

"Sex slave?" Dev repeats with a chuckle. "Way to go boss-man."

"Damn, it must be good to be the prez," Silas says with a rare smile.

"Does that mean I can fuck her again now?" Fiasco asks.

"No, man. You can't. And you never fucked her. She sucked you off to get a job so she could steal from us for Harry fucking Cox," I say, lowering my hands from my head to sit up straight when I call him out.

"She stole from us?" Dev asks.

"Yeah, fifteen K from us and customers to pay off a debt she owes to Harry. But I'm going to put the money back and repay anyone missing shit since she and I worked out an alternative repayment plan," I explain.

"And that alternative plan includes her riding your dick?" Fiasco grumbles.

"Yeah, it does. Whenever I want, twenty-four hours a fucking day."

"You're an evil genius," Dev chuckles.

"If she was stealing from the MC, then we should all get to gang bang her twenty-four seven as part of your repayment plan," Fiasco says.

"The fuck did you just say?" I snap at him.

"She stole from the Aces, so all six of us should get a few turns with her," he repeats, making my teeth grit together in annoyance. "At least let us vote on it to see who wants a turn."

Son of a bitch.

He's serious about sharing her, passing her around like a joint. Guess I should've kept the part about her owing the club money to myself and just put it all back. And knowing how hardheaded Fiasco is, he's not going to let this go until we do have a table vote where any of my other brothers may start thinking they should get a turn too. That's never going to fucking happen. But I can't just shut him down since this is now a club issue.

"Tell you what, *Phillip*," I start, using his real name that I know he hates, when I come up with an idea. "How about me and you get in the cage one-on-one tomorrow night. If you beat me, you can have her. If I win, you can never say another goddamn thing about her, and you sure as shit will never lay another finger on her."

The room turns completely silent as the weight of my words sinks in.

"*Fuuuck,*" Silas mutters. "It's been a long time since we've had a good fight." Turning to Dev, he says, "I've got a grand on our prez taking Fi out in the first round."

"I'm not stupid enough to take that bet," Dev responds with a roll of his eyes.

"What do you say, Fiasco?" I ask since he's still quiet and unusually thoughtful, so much so his forehead is all wrinkled up. "You gonna put your money where your mouth is?"

Finally, he grins at me. "It's funny you should say that. It's the exact same line I asked Naomi before she got down on her knees and I shoved my dick down her throat."

"Just answer the goddamn question," I growl, hating that visual image more than I've ever hated any fucking thing. That right there should've been my first clue that I've lost my shit for a thieving piece of ass with a banging body and a pretty face.

"A fight for a two-week fuck fest with Naomi? Count me in," Fiasco agrees. "As long as there won't be any hard feelings when I kick your ass, prez."

"What happens in the cage stays in the cage," I assure him when I hold out my palm for him to come and shake on it.

"Deal," he agrees as he takes it and squeezes my fingers like that'll make me scared of him.

There's no fucking way I'm going to lose this fight. There's too much at stake, and I'll be damned if I'm going to give up Naomi before I've even gotten started on the long list of depraved things I've thought about doing to her.

CHAPTER ELEVEN

Naomi

"Holy crap. Your house is...small," I say as I take in the one-bedroom beach house on stilts. I struggle to climb off the back off his bike, until Malcolm grabs my arm to steady me.

"Is that a bad thing? Were you expecting a mansion?" Malcolm questions me. Snaking his arm around my waist and running his tongue up the side of my neck, he goes on to ask, "Is it only big houses and piles of money that get your pussy nice and wet?"

"No," I tell him honestly since his mouth is all it takes to get me wet.

"Yeah, sure," he mutters. "Don't think I haven't figured out why you only gave Fiasco a blowjob but are going to let me fuck you as much as I want. He's broke and the low man on the totem pole; I'm not."

"That doesn't matter to me," I say as I step away from his hands and mouth to turn and face him. "And in case you forgot, you're the one who came up with this arrangement where I'm your whore."

"Right," he drawls sarcastically with a roll of his eyes. "Just don't get too attached. After two weeks, your ass is out of here. If I wanted a live-in girlfriend or wife, I would've bought one already."

"Bought one?" I scoff. "Wow, you're so romantic, Malcolm."

"Just speaking the truth," he replies with a shrug of his shoulders. "Money gets you into panties."

"It's not just about money. Do I think it's sexy when a man earns a living and supports himself? Hell yes. What woman doesn't? But that's not all there is in the world..."

"Okay, honey. If you say so. I've had enough talking for tonight, though. Why don't you go get naked and get in my bed?" Grabbing my shoulder, he spins me around and points straight ahead. "It's right at the end of that hall, big four-poster king bed. Can't miss it."

After he walks off, I wander into the bedroom and debate sprawling naked on his bed as he asked or defying him.

A big, powerful man like Malcolm probably enjoys the thrill of the chase, not having women throw themselves at him constantly, making it too easy. That must be why he always turned down his employees.

Well, before me, that is...

I'm still not sure why he finally broke his rule for me. There must have been women a lot prettier than me, curvier with bigger boobs and a lot more experience. Still, I would be lying if I said that I'm not looking forward to the next two weeks. I'm thrilled that *I'm* Malcolm's exception. It makes me feel...special. Sure, I had to agree to let him use my body whenever he wants, however he wants, in order to get out of my mess with Harry; but based on my experience in Malcolm's office, I'm going to thoroughly enjoy being his to command. Already, my tummy is tightening at the prospect of being dominated by him again. Still, I don't plan to let him know just how much I want him or make it too easy for him to get inside of me.

Next to Malcolm's big bed (that I have no doubt has seen more pussy than most gynecologists) is a matching cherry wood dresser. I head straight for it, opening one drawer after another until I find a stack of folded cotton t-shirts. None look brand new. Most are thin and some have holes in them like they've been well loved over many years. I pull an old black one out and slip it over my head before rummaging around until I find Malcolm's boxer briefs. They'll probably be a little big on me, but I pull a pair on anyway. After I roll the elastic top down a few times, they finally stay put.

Now what the heck am I supposed to do?

Before I can figure out a plan, I hear Malcolm's heavy boots coming closer and then his wide shoulders are filling the narrow doorway, a bottle of beer in each of his hands. He silently stares at me with his jaw tight, apparently not appreciating the fact that I went through his things already. Finally, he goes over and sits the drinks down on the nightstand before turning back to me. "What the hell are you wearing?" he asks.

"Your shirt and boxers," I say as I glance down, thinking that should be obvious since all I had on when we came in was a torn dress and panties.

"Take them off," he says as he turns back over to the table and pops the caps on the bottles. Picking one up, he takes a big swig.

"No," I reply without thinking.

For a second there, I thought he was going to choke on his beer. He doesn't, though. He just silently drinks it while I wait for his reaction, making me envious of the bottle who has taken up all his attention.

Eventually, he lowers the beer and starts to remove his leather vest. Passing by me as if I don't exist, he opens the closet door and walks inside. When he comes back out a moment later, his shirt is also missing, flaunting his bare chest with a dusting of hair down the center and washboard abs in front of me for the first time. And damn, does he look even better without the clothing. I gasp when my eyes lower to his outie belly button, unable to figure out why something so innocent causes dampness between my legs. My mouth waters, and I quickly swallow it down. How is it possible that Malcolm has a sexy belly button of all damn things on top of all of his other attributes?

"Did you forget the conversation we had earlier when I was balls deep inside of you?" he asks, his words distracting me from his body. Instead of coming straight for me as I half expected, he stays several feet away. "I'm the one who gives the orders. You do what I say for the next two weeks."

I lean my back against the wall next to his dresser and cross my arms over my chest, waiting.

"Are you seriously trying to test me?" Malcolm asks. "We had a deal. And trust me, Naomi, you really don't want to fuck around with me again."

My entire body freezes as soon as my name leaves his lips. He says it like he owns it, owns me. And my traitorous body is already being trained to his voice. It's eager to obey him and only him.

When Malcolm stalks toward me, I have no idea what he's gonna do to me. My pulse rises the closer he gets, and my eyes get distracted again by his naked upper body that's covered in tattoos except for the fuzzy line trailing down into his jeans. I may have even licked my lips at the sight, but then he's towering above me, only inches away. I almost moan when he grabs the bottom of the t-shirt I'm wearing and balls it up tightly in his fist.

"So, are you going to be my fuck doll for fourteen days, or do you want to take your chances with Harry?" he asks, his warm breath ghosting over my cheek, smelling of beer.

I drag my eyes up his chiseled stomach and chest to his face to answer, but his green eyes are intoxicating from this distance. Before, when Malcolm fucked me in his office, he stayed behind me the entire time. But now, looking into the depths of eyes that are blazing with a demanding authority, I know how he became the president of the Dirty Aces. I also know that I'll do anything he wants and maybe even beg for it.

His gaze continues to hold mine while his calloused palm glides over my hips and slips down into the back of his boxers I'm wearing, cupping my ass before jerking the cotton down my legs.

My shirt is then yanked up. And when I raise my arms to assist in the removal, Malcolm restrains them both above my head on the wall.

"Let me explain something to you," he whispers in my ear before dipping his tongue inside, making me squirm with need. He steps forward, using the front of his body to keep me still, and boy does it when I feel his cock hard and thick against my thigh. "We. Made. A. Deal. So every time you refuse me, you'll be punished before I fuck you."

"You-you should probably know that I have a bit of a stubborn streak," I tell him as I lick my lips that have gone dry. "And I'm a slow learner."

He arches one eyebrow, and his lips almost quirk up at the meaning behind my words. "So you like to play rough?"

"A little rough can be fun sometimes."

"Good, because I have a lot of rough fucks to give you. Starting now."

This time there's definitely a smirk on his handsome face when he releases my hands to grab both of my ass cheeks. Hefting me up off my feet and around his waist, Malcolm carries me to the bed. As soon as he tosses me to the center of the mattress, his massive body is covering mine, pinning me down so that even exhaling is a feat. Malcolm's mouth seals over one of my nipples a second later, sucking hard and making me writhe in the confined space underneath him.

This is just a business deal, paying him back after he caught me stealing. I shouldn't want his mouth on me or any other part of him, but I can't help myself. My back arches off the mattress at the same time an embarrassing moan escapes past my lips. How long has it been since a man's touched me like this, so aggressively and without apology?

The truth is, it's *never* been like this before.

Malcolm's teeth bite into the meaty flesh of my breast until I cry out at the sudden jolt of pain and try to get away. That only makes him chuckle harder before his mouth lowers, his tongue dipping into my belly button, sending a pleasurable jolt all through my body.

"Oh God," I groan, and instinctively my hands search for something to hold on to, something to anchor me while my body demands that his mouth moves lower. My fingers dive into Malcolm's thick, brown waves and tug hard, telling him what I want but not being able to find the words to say. His hair feels even better than I expected.

"Easy there, honey. I'll eat your pussy when I'm good and ready," he says when his searing green eyes peek up at me in warning. "Just for that, now I'm gonna take my time."

"Hurry up! Please," I beg, and I never, ever beg, but this man has got me so hot that I can't wait any longer.

"I think you need a reminder of who's in charge here," Malcolm says before he suddenly rolls off the bed, leaving me lying there, sweaty, desperate and needy. Watching him walk around the room only amplifies that desire. His long hair is now ruffled by my fingers running through it, and his kissable full lips are red and full from sucking on my flesh. When he opens a drawer on the nightstand and pulls out something metal, it takes my sex hazed mind longer than usual to realize they're two pairs of handcuffs.

"W-wait, what are you doing?" I ask, sitting up on my elbows. "You're not putting those on me," I tell him. When his eyes narrow, I know I've said the wrong thing. Or maybe the right one?

Before I can scramble away on all fours, he's on me, an arm wrapped around my waist, dragging me back to the center of the bed on my stomach. I can barely breathe when he presses all his weight on my backside, holding me down while he grabs for my wrists. I try to buck him off, but he's twice my size and stronger than a freaking ox. The metal clicks tightly over one wrist and then the other, and then I'm his.

Why does the idea of being his, combined with his weight

bearing down on me, dominating me, get me so wet that the arousal may very well leave a puddle in his bed soon?

Malcolm is not even out of breath when he flips me over and pulls me by the chain connecting the two cuffs to the headboard. A second later, my arms are raised and there's another metallic click. I try to lower my arms, but they only come to my forehead before they meet resistance.

"There," Malcolm says. "Now, where were we?" he asks before his palms grasp both of my knees and spreads them wide apart. "Oh right. You were begging me to lick your pussy."

"Was not," I counter.

"So you weren't trying to scalp me when you were moaning *please?*"

In response to his question, I exhale heavily, trying to blow my sweaty hair out of my eyes and then remain silent.

"If you've forgotten already, I'd be happy to remind you," Malcolm says before his head lowers between my legs. His wet tongue licks a straight line from my knee down up my inner thigh, stopping right where I want his tongue. I try not to squirm, to not let his ministrations get to me, even when he blows the cool air from his mouth over my pussy. A small giggle escapes, and then it's like a dam bursting as my body shakes with laughter.

"What the fuck are you laughing at?" Malcom sits back on his knees and asks.

Tears leak down my cheeks, so it's hard to see the expression on his face. And since my hands are restrained, I can't even wipe them away.

"You just gave me a *blow* job," I tell him, followed by another giggle.

"Are you high or drunk?" he asks.

"No," I reply. "I'm handcuffed to the bed of a man who caught me stealing from him hours ago, a man Harry said would kill me if I got caught."

"Did you really think for a second that I would kill you?" he asks, putting his hands on his hips and sounding genuinely annoyed.

"Seriously? Um, I dunno."

"Well, in that case, I don't know what's more fucked up – the fact that you think I could kill so easily or the fact that you're in my bed begging me to tongue fuck you despite the fact that you think you're in mortal jeopardy."

"I-I wasn't begging."

"You were," he says, lowering himself over me until his face is inches from mine, those hypnotic eyes burning into my blue ones. "And if you really thought I would kill you or harm you, I don't think you would have ever let me touch you."

"But Harry will if I don't pay him the rest of his money."

"I'm going to take care of that asshole. But right now, there's nothing we can do about it tonight. Since you're naked in my bed and begging me to lick your tight little pussy, I'm going to fuck you as many times as I can get my dick up and deal with him tomorrow."

"I didn't beg...*oh God!*" I exclaim when Malcolm suddenly shoves one of his thick fingers inside me.

"You did, and you will again," he says before he leans down to take one of my nipples between his teeth and tug on it before applying suction. Between that and the hand between my legs while my arms are restrained, it doesn't take long before every inch of my body ignites into flames that threaten to burn me from the inside out. Just as soon as Malcolm's mouth lowers and his tongue starts to flutter against my clit, I combust, coming apart in waves of pleasure so intense they almost hurt.

By the time the fire slowly dies down inside of me, Malcolm's damp chest is right above my face as he rhythmically rolls his hips like he's moving to the most erotic song ever. On each upward thrust, he relentlessly fills me with his long, hard as steel flesh over and over again. At some point, my legs wrapped around his waist, so that my heels are digging into his muscular ass, urging him to go deeper even though there's not a breath of space inside me that he hasn't thoroughly plundered.

My mouth goes dry from the various gasps and moans I'm making, so I lap up Malcolm's slick skin as his pecs move back and forth over my tongue. He tastes delicious, salty with a hint of coconut.

"Fuck, Naomi," he says, my name rolling off his tongue like a familiar lover instead of a near stranger. Lowering himself to his forearms puts his neck within reach of my lips, so I devour that skin as well. Malcolm must like it, because he growls against my ear and then loses his rhythm, his massive body shuddering after he rams his cock as far as it will go inside me one final time.

Once he goes still, his brick wall of a chest grazes mine with each of our panting breaths, and his gasps are loud next to my ear where his wet lips are still pressed, tickling me, making me squirm underneath him since I can't push him away. I'm not sure I really want to.

Malcolm abruptly grabs both sides of my jaw in one of his strong hands, squeezing it in a tight grip so that I'm forced to meet his gaze. His eyes are heavy lidded and there's a hint of a smile trying to tip the corners of his bearded lips, so I know he's not angry. "The next time I come, it's gonna be in this sexy mouth, and it'll be your fault for teasing me with it."

"You taste good," I tell him, obviously still high on endorphins. Now, he does smile down at me for the very first time, and he's so gorgeous he takes my breath away.

"So do you," he replies before he rolls away and climbs off the bed. The loss of him between my legs leaves me feeling empty. My inner walls spasm as if searching for Malcolm, missing the way he stretches and fills up the space like he was made for it.

I follow his movements across the room, eyeing his semi-erect cock and ready to beg him for it again, even though I don't beg. It's a relief to see there's a condom covering his big Johnson, although I have no idea when he took the time to put it on. Without a word, he disappears into the bathroom where I hear water running, his shower

I'm guessing. Eventually, clouds of steam come rolling out, smelling of sweet, delicious coconuts and sandalwood. It must be his body wash or shampoo that gives him the mouthwatering scent.

    I can't believe he left me handcuffed to his bed while he went to take a freaking shower. Still, other than wishing I was covered with sheets and my arms were free, I'm surprisingly content. In fact, in no time at all, my eyes drift closed, and I let my body relax into the mattress.

CHAPTER TWELVE

Malcolm

Stupid. What I'm doing with Naomi is incredibly stupid. The fact that I know full well it's stupid yet I'm still doing it makes me a fucking idiot. I'm usually smarter than this, less spontaneous and more thoughtful, calculated in everything I do.

Naomi has a way of throwing me off balance, forcing me to just react and not think. In a way, it's freeing; but it's also dangerous.

Under the warm stream of the shower is where it hits me that tomorrow night, I'm going head to head in an actual three round fight with my own MC brother, a man who has a significant height and weight advantage on me, all for a thief. A thief who happens to be sexy as fuck and that I can't seem to resist no matter how hard I try. To top it off, tomorrow I've volunteered to be punched, kicked, and most likely beaten bloody for her.

Since it's too late to change my mind now, I slick my wet hair back from my face, wring out as much water as I can, and then grab a towel from the rack to start drying off.

I know it was a dick move to leave Naomi restrained to my bed while I showered, but she deserves a little retribution for turning me into a possessive caveman for the first time in my life, one who has started making incredibly bad decisions.

As soon as there are no longer droplets of water dripping down my body, I toss the towel into the hamper and go back to the bedroom to let my captive go.

I was expecting to be met with the glare of Naomi's angry, blue eyes for leaving her restrained. Instead, her head is flopped to one side, a few blonde strands of hair hanging in front of her closed eyes. Her pink lips are parted as she sleeps soundly with her arms still stretched above her head.

She looks like a goddamn fallen angel I lucked up and captured by accident. I knew from day one that she didn't belong in my world. The proof that I shouldn't trust her was a slap in the face just a few days ago, and still I brought her home with me, the only woman I've ever brought back to my home.

I always prefer to handle my dick's business at a hookup's house because I don't want them knowing where I live, showing up whenever they want, asking me for shit. I deal with enough needy bitches at the bar and on the boat. I don't want to deal with it at home. Not that I'm here very often, no more than a few hours to sleep most days, before getting back to work at the clubhouse.

From out of nowhere, it hits me that, if I had Naomi waiting for me in my bed every night, I sure as shit would make more time to be home.

Retrieving the tiny metal key from the same drawer I keep the handcuffs in, I crawl up on the bed and get to work on undoing them. The movements cause Naomi's eyes to blink open and look up at me as I work.

"Mmm. About time," she mumbles. "Thought you were gonna leave me like this all night."

"Thought about it," I tease her. "But my dick has to rest some time."

"Ha-ha," she retorts softly as I release her wrists and lower her arms. She immediately rolls to her side, curling up in a ball like she's cold. Probably is, since there's not a stitch of fabric on her and my air conditioning runs full blast in the summer. I cover her up with the comforter and then pull my jeans back on to head out back for a smoke.

The sounds of the waves crashing just a few feet away in the dark night are just as calming and relaxing as usual. It's one of the reasons I refuse to sell this place for something bigger. In a world that's usually chaotic, this is my peace.

And for whatever reason, knowing Naomi is here, waiting for me in my bed makes it feel even more like paradise.

Naomi

I can count on one hand how many times I've woken up next to a sleeping man. Usually the first emotion I feel is regret.

Not this morning.

I wake up in the comfiest bed, with the softest linens, with a bearded and inked muscular man sleeping naked beside me. I'm not sure it gets any better than this. Again, it makes me think that I'm getting a much better deal here than Malcolm.

I don't regret stealing from Malcolm, and I sure as shit don't regret agreeing to this deal with him, having the best sex of my life while being done with Harry. Or at least Malcolm claims he'll take care of my debt...

Currently, the man in charge of my body for the next two weeks is lying sound asleep on his back, covers thrown off all but one of his thick legs. A single tattooed arm is thrown above his head, the other is resting on his bare pelvis, his fingers incredibly close to the base of his dick that's long, hard and proud, raring to go before its master even opens his eyes.

Unable to resist, I reach over and wrap my fingers around his veiny girth and give it a stroke. Malcolm said the next time he comes he wants it to be in my mouth. And, at the moment, I can't think of a better way to start the morning since my body is still humming from the orgasms he gave me last night.

On the second rough stroke, Malcolm makes a throaty rumbling sound like a dangerous, wild beast...right before he grabs my hand and peels it from his cock.

"Not now, honey," he says with annoyance in his voice, as if I'm trying to floss his teeth while he sleeps rather than give him what was going to be a very enjoyable blowjob.

"I think your dick disagrees," I tell him when the appendage twitches and grows impossibly longer.

Malcolm's deep green eyes are barely open, just narrowed slits that are watching me. "Can't come again until after tonight. Gotta save up my load before the fight."

"A fight? Seriously?" He must be joking.

"Seriously."

"What does coming have to do with a fight?" I ask in confusion.

"Getting off too much makes men lazy, way too complacent. Need the testosterone and hunger."

When he doesn't elaborate, I ask, "Is this fight of yours going to take place on the playground after dark?"

"No." Malcolm stretches both of his arms above his head, then grips the headboard behind him, making it shake and his biceps bulge. "It'll be in the cage out behind the bar."

I think he's actually telling the truth. This crazy man is going to have a bare fisted brawl with someone, which blows my mind. "And who will you be fighting in this cage behind the bar?"

"Fiasco."

"Fiasco?" I repeat in surprise. "Why are you fighting Fiasco?"

With an exasperated sigh, Malcolm rolls out of bed and grabs a pair of clean jeans from a drawer, then pulls them up his legs. After tucking his erection down into them and zipping up, he finally props his hands on his hips to answer me. "Fiasco wanted me to share you with him for the next two weeks. I said no, and he wasn't going to just let it go. So, we're gonna fight to see who gets to have you."

"Excuse me?" I ask, sitting up straight in bed.

The infuriating man doesn't immediately respond. He's too busy fetching a lighter and a pack of smokes from his dresser and then opening the bedroom window.

"Malcolm!" I shout at him, but it doesn't do any good.

He doesn't speak again until the cigarette is lit and he's taken his first deep pull from it. Once he blows the smoke out, he finally says, "If I win, Fiasco will get the fuck over you. But if I lose..."

"What? If you lose, *what*?" I demand.

Speaking around the smoke between his lips, he says, "Then you're his for the next two weeks."

I'm his. I'm *his*?

Oh hell no!

"Malcolm! You can't be serious!" When he doesn't respond, I scoff indignantly and then jump out of bed to start putting my clothes on before I remember I don't have any clothes at his house. He shredded my dress, and I didn't even have a change of underwear with me! "How-how dare you offer me up like I'm your property!" I yell as I find and pull up his boxer briefs I wore last night for about two minutes before he tore them off me. "I agreed to be your whore, not his!"

"I thought I was the whore," the asshole responds with a smirk. "And don't worry. I'm not going to lose."

"How do you know that?" I shriek. Malcolm may be tough, but Fiasco has a very noticeable size advantage on him.

"Just trust me, honey," he mutters, more concerned with his cigarette than my fury.

"And if you're wrong? What then?" I ask him as I spin around, looking for something to cover up the rest of my body since I refuse to put the piece of shredded dress back on. I finally find Malcolm's discarded shirt I had on last night. "Am I supposed to just leave your bed for *his*? How could you do this to me?"

"Fiasco had a point," he answers coolly with smoke blowing from his nose like an angry dragon. "The debt you owe is to the MC. A fight seemed the fairest way to decide who you repay for two weeks."

"You could've just told him no, that you wouldn't give me up!" I shout at him.

"If I made an exception for you, everything else I do while I'm in charge will be seen as partial. I can't afford to lose the trust of my brothers, or the entire MC will fall apart."

He can't be serious! Keeping his precious *authority* is more important than I am to him?

"Oh, so you would rather just let your MC brother have me without even bothering to ask me what I wanted?" I huff.

"You've already sucked his dick, so it's not like it'll be all new territory."

Unable to deal with this conversation or revelation for another second, I stalk to the bathroom, telling him, "You're a dick, Malcolm!" before I slam the door and lock it.

"Does that mean I won't see you at the fight tonight?" the jackass has the nerve to yell through the door.

I just can't even with this man!

Who does he think he is, giving me away like I'm not a person with actual feelings? Yes, I'm guilty of stealing from him, and I do wish there had been any other option, but there wasn't! And maybe I also stupidly thought that Malcolm had a soft spot for me, when really, he's just an evil, horny bastard who cares more about his reputation than me, an actual woman.

Malcolm

It's probably for the best that Naomi doesn't want to come to the fight tonight. Seeing her ringside would be a distraction I sure as fuck don't need.

Do I think I can beat Fiasco?

Hell yes.

But there is no denying that the jackass has at least twenty pounds on me and a few inches of arm reach. I'll just have to be the smarter fighter, which should be easy since Fiasco's an idiot who makes terrible fucking decisions on a regular basis. I swear he treats being a dumbass like it's his job.

If he hadn't hired Naomi in exchange for a blowjob, she wouldn't have stolen from us, and I wouldn't have developed an unhealthy obsession with her. One that is now affecting how I run shit as president.

It's too damn early to even be up this morning; but as soon as Naomi grabbed my dick, I went from sound asleep to wide the fuck awake.

Of course I wanted her to jerk it, suck it, ride it, any or all of the above, but most fighters swear that abstaining right before a fight is key to keeping their edge. And I'm going to need every advantage I can get.

CHAPTER THIRTEEN

Naomi

"How did you do it?" Anika asks me in the employee lounge as soon as we board the boat.

"What?"

"How did you do it? How did you get Malcolm to fuck you? You're not even that hot."

Wow. Jealous much?

"It's really none of your business or anyone else's," I tell her, even though I have no idea who told her. Maybe no one had to after the romp we had in his office...

"He's fighting Fiasco for her tonight," Ronnie interjects when she comes out of the bathroom, having apparently heard our conversation through the door.

"Bullshit!" Anika exclaims.

"It's true. I heard some of the guys talking about it in the bar last night," Ronnie answers.

"For her? What do you mean *for* her?" Anika repeats with a jab of her thumb in my direction.

"Whoever wins gets to have her," Ronnie explains.

"Sounds like you're both just jealous," Chloe, the normally quiet weekend only waitress, says to them.

"I'm not jealous," Ronnie remarks. "They're treating her like she's property they can pass around. Probably will too. Malcolm's only interested in her because, as the club's president, he can't afford to look like a loser. She's not that special. It's nothing but a testosterone-fueled pissing contest."

"Two grown-ass men are going to fist fight each other for her when they could both have any other girl they wanted with just the snap of their fingers," Chloe remarks. "Including you two. Like it or not, Naomi is obviously special to have two hot men go to such extremes."

I mouth a thank you to the only woman sticking up for me, and Chloe gives me a wink before she saunters back onto the casino floor. Neither of the other women say another word after she's gone either.

But Ronnie is right. I don't feel special. I feel like an object, a toy that Malcolm and Fiasco are arguing over only because the other one has been with me. They don't care about my thoughts or feelings on the issue. All they're thinking with is their possessive dicks, which is incredibly immature.

It would serve Malcolm right to get his ass kicked. God, I bet the Dirty Aces president would be so embarrassed if Fiasco knocked him out in front of everyone.

Still, for some stupid reason, I want Malcolm to win.

∼

Malcolm

"You ready for tonight?" Nash comes into my office on the boat and asks around midnight.

"I wouldn't have suggested it if I wasn't," I remark.

"This girl has got you twisted, prez," he says with a shake of his head.

"I'm fighting to make a point, not for her. Besides, you're one to talk about being twisted over a girl. Do you even let yourself look at other women, or are you afraid Ellie would consider that cheating if she were to ever find out?"

"That's different," he says. "She's my wife. I still have an obligation to her."

"Don't you think it's time to file for divorce?" I ask him. "She's been gone for years."

"Sort of hard to send her papers if I don't know where the fuck she is," he grumbles.

"Have you hired a PI?" When he doesn't answer my question, I assume he hasn't. He's afraid of what he'll find her doing if and when he locates her. His wife has no doubt moved on, regardless of their legal status.

"Right now we're talking about you acting like a dumbass for a woman, not me," Nash huffs to change the subject.

"It is what it is with Naomi," I tell him. "I happen to like fucking her, and you know how I feel about sharing – I don't."

"That's all this is?" he asks with his arms crossed over his chest.

"Yep. That's it."

The jewelry box in my jean pocket suddenly feels heavy, squeezing my leg like the blood pressure cuff on a polygraph machine. I know damned well I'm lying to Nash, and myself. If Naomi was just a good fuck, why did I feel the ridiculous urge to buy her diamonds to try and bribe her to forgive me after the fallout we had this morning? She was really fucking pissed at me, and I...hated it.

No, I didn't just hate it. There's been an actual gnawing ache in my stomach like a burning ulcer ever since Naomi left my house without a word. I'm not entirely sure if she'll come back tonight or not, despite our deal. If she doesn't, at least I know where she lives so I can go haul her ass back. Or at least give her this trinket I bought for her before I came to work tonight while I try and apologize. Jesus, what the hell is wrong with me?

"Are you absolutely fucking sure?" Nash asks. "Because now with the expansion and shit about to go down, it would be a bad time for you to lose your mind for some piece of ass."

"You fucking know me. The MC comes first. Always has and always will," I tell him. "And that's the end of this fucking conversation."

"Whatever you say, prez," he mutters. "So what are you going to do about that bastard Harry Cox? He's the reason you said Naomi stole from us, right?"

"Yeah, he's the reason," I agree. "And I've got a plan for him. Instead of revenge, I'm thinking this could be a time for negotiations."

"Negotiations?" Nash repeats. "Is that a code word for fucking him up?"

"I would love nothing more than to knock that fat fuck's lights out," I reply. "But no. You're all about wanting the MC to expand, right? Patching over a few clubs is the first step. The second is coming up with a way to increase profits for all of us."

"And you trust Harry enough to do business with the fucker?"

"No, I don't trust him or his daughter as far as I could throw the tub of lard, but that doesn't mean we can't carefully use his connections to make some serious cash for us and the new guys."

"Expansion over revenge?" Nash asks with a hint of a grin lifting his lips. "I like it. No matter how much we hate the bastard, it's about time we start thinking shit through instead of flying off the handle over every little thing."

"Lowell was always the hot head who got us in too deep more times than I can count," I remind him.

"True. He was an impulsive son of a bitch," he agrees with a grin. "God rest his soul."

"We're all getting too old to pull that kind of shit. It's time to take the Aces in a new direction, one with less bloodshed and more cash in our pockets."

"Finally!" Nash laughs. "I guess the girl hasn't got you in a complete pussy fog."

"A pussy fog?" I huff.

"You better win tonight," he remarks as he starts for the door. "If you don't, Fiasco will never let you live it down."

"I know," I grumble. "You think I can take him?" I ask.

"Depends on how good the pussy is. Guess we're all going to find out," Nash answers with a smirk before walking out of my office.

In other words, he doesn't think I can beat Fiasco in a fair fight, not unless I'm absolutely fucking ruthless.

∽

Even though we bring the boat in early tonight, it's still almost two a.m. when we all rumble back to the clubhouse. All of the Aces are here along with our employees and most of the club girls. There are even some prospective members from other clubs we're considering patching over.

I wave Nash over as soon as I get off my bike. "Let's get this over with. Make sure Fiasco understands the terms. Three rounds, three minutes each. If there's no clear winner, we keep going until it's settled. No other rules."

"No other rules?" Nash protests. "Fiasco has got fifty pounds on you, man! You sure you don't want to at least..."

"No other rules," I interrupt him. "I don't want him claiming he lost on some technicality and whining about this shit later. Besides, he can't remember more than two things at a time. He'd forget any rules we set before we start."

"All right," Nash agrees as he turns away. "This is going to be a fucking train wreck," he mutters under his breath as he walks towards our audience. "We start in five, everyone!" he roars above the din of conversation. "Fiasco, get your ass into the cage and get ready!"

I take off my cut and t-shirt, laying them over the seat of my bike before I head over to the cage behind our clubhouse. While I wait outside the chain-link gate, I dig a cigarette out of the half-crushed pack in the pocket of my jeans, lighting it up before I start taking off my belt. I throw my wallet, knife, and smokes on the ground along with the belt, then concentrate on my cigarette as the crowd gathers and Fiasco gets ready on the other side of the cage, removing all his shit too.

Once Nash leads Fiasco through the gate opposite me, he waves me to come on in. I drop my smoke and grind it under my boot, then climb into the cage with the two men. Nash doesn't bother with any fancy announcements or any sort of ceremony. Everyone gathered here knows what this is about, and why we're squaring off.

"Anything you two want to say to each other before we get started?" Nash asks as I approach.

"Yeah," Fiasco grunts. "I fucking hate this, but I fucking hate a hypocrite even more. Being president doesn't mean you get to live by a different set of rules than the rest of us. We elected you because you're smart, and you were fair. I'm gonna make sure you remember that by beating it into your stubborn head."

"You're right," I tell Fiasco. I can't help but crack a smile at the confusion in his narrowed eyes as he takes a step back. "I've been a hypocrite about Naomi. I made up a rule so everyone would leave her alone and you wouldn't fuck with her while I tried to sort out how I feel about her. She's got me knotted up a bit, but she's the only thing fucking with me right now. Nothing about that girl or about how I deal with her is going to bring any trouble to the club."

"You're goddamn right it isn't," Fiasco scoffs. "'Cuz I'm going to smack you around and then go take her back to my place, get her out of your hair permanently. She's causing fucking problems, and if you can't see it, I'll have to beat you until your vision clears up."

"I've warned you too many times about thinking with your dick, Fiasco. You might have yourself convinced you're doing something noble for the club, but we both know what you're after here." I don't even recognize the growl that has become my voice as I feel the jealous rage building up inside of me. "You will *never* lay another hand on that woman. I admitted I made a mistake in how I dealt with her and the club. I should have been more specific from the start. No one fucking touches Naomi except for me." Turning to the crowd, I raise my voice to roar at the rest of the gathered Aces. "She's mine, and if any of you sons-of-bitches have a mind to test me, I'll shut your whore mouths just like I'm going to shut his!" I jab a finger at Fiasco as I finish, then turn my back on him as I stomp across the cage.

"Well, I guess that's it for the talking," Nash comments. "On my signal, fight!" he yells, right before he toots an air horn he has clutched in his fist. He leaps backwards as Fiasco and I rush each other.

I hear a cheer go up from the crowd gathered around the cage right before I'm deafened by Fiasco's fist to my ear. I managed to block most of the punch and twist away from him, but the impact still rattled me down to my knees. He doesn't let up at all, throwing haymakers that I have to leap away from, twisting and dodging while covering my head until he wears himself out.

This idea of mine, fighting Fiasco for three rounds, sounded a lot better in my head. Now that he's actually nailing me with his fists like he's got something to prove, I'm starting to think I may have fucked up. I can feel a trickle of blood from my ear; and while I'm managing to stay just out of his reach, seconds that stretch into eternity pass with him showing no signs of slowing down or getting tired. It's all I can do to avoid getting hammered into the ground by the big bastard, and the only punches I've been able to land seem to just bounce off his thick skull.

When Nash finally blows the air horn again minutes or years later, I stagger backwards as Fiasco throws his hands into the air.

"That's what you get, president bitch!" he roars, stomping back to the other side of the cage.

"Watch your mouth, Fiasco," Nash cautions him. "Don't be disrespectful or escalate this beyond this fight. You okay?" he asks, turning his attention to me as I lean on the cage, gasping for air.

"Yeah, yeah, I'm fine," I reassure him with a wave. "Just waiting for him to gas out, you know, the old rope-a-dope, that sort of thing," I manage to chuckle.

"He's not going to get tired," Nash frowns at me. "You know how long he's worked for that construction company. He's been swinging a hammer all day for years. That's before he comes out and bounces drunks on the boat at night. You're ten years older and a whole lotta pounds lighter than him. Jesus, Malcolm, how did you think this was going to go?"

"This fight ain't fucking over yet," I grit out. "Toot your little goddamn horn and stay out of the way, Nash. I can only be the president as long as I earn it. I fucked up, and now I'm going to set it right."

"By letting Fiasco murder you?" Nash scoffs.

"Blow your horn and shut up," I growl as I march back to the center of the ring.

Nash complies, and just as he predicted, Fiasco is back on me again in an instant. He rushes in with another haymaker; and after watching him in the first round, I can see that swinging for the fences seems to be his go-to move. This time, I duck under his arm easily, twisting back to punch him in the kidney, and then hit him again in his belly, driving my fist up as hard as I can.

The move works, sort of. Fiasco staggers to the side with an explosion of breath, his mouth moving wordlessly as he tries to find the air to cuss. He clenches his belly as he swings a huge backhand at me, which I easily jump back from. I knocked the wind out of him, but when my fist met his stomach, my wrist popped, sending a bolt of pain all the way up my arm. Hitting his abs felt like punching a brick wall, and from the numbness in my hand, I'm not sure who got the worst of the exchange.

I change tactics again since I can't feel my right hand, rushing forward as Fiasco straightens and slamming my elbow into his chin. His head rocks back; but instead of staggering backwards, he lunges towards me, wrapping one of his massive arms around my neck. He pulls me downward until I'm almost completely bent over, and then uses his free hand to swing upward, trying to strike my face.

I manage to get my hands in the way to block most of the blows; but no matter how I twist my neck, I can't break free of his headlock. I kick at his leg, trying to take him to the ground, but I might as well be trying to kick down an oak tree. His arm squeezes my neck like a python with a body odor problem, stifling my breath. In desperation, I spread my hands in front of my face; and as Fiasco takes the opportunity to ram a punch into my face, I grab at his fist and use both hands to spread his fingers open. As soon as I manage to loosen his fist, I grab his pinky finger; and with every ounce of strength I can muster, I twist it away from his hand.

"FUCK!" Fiasco screeches as he lets go of my neck, dropping me to one knee as he releases me and practically runs to the other side of the cage. Shaking his injured hand, he holds it up to show everyone that his pinky finger is now sticking out perpendicular to the rest of his digits. "You cheap-ass bitch!" he roars as he grabs the dislocated finger, jerking it back into position with a stifled sob. He leans back against the cage wall as I regain my feet, pushing my hair back out of my face.

"We are the *Dirty* Aces, remember?" I mutter as I spit out a line of blood from my busted lip. "I told you I was going to fuck you up," I remind him.

"You nasty mother-fucker..." Fiasco snarls as he steps forward, just before Nash blows his horn.

"That's round two!" Nash calls. "Can you continue?" he asks, nodding towards Fiasco.

"You're damned right I can," he agrees as he shakes his injured hand. "I don't punch with my pinky. Tear it off, next time, I'll just shove it up your ass!"

"Okay," Nash says, rolling his eyes as he turns towards me. "You're looking a little worse for wear, prez. You still in for round three?"

"I know how this fucking looks," I reply. "It looks like I'm getting my ass kicked."

"Yeah, it does. If you don't put Fiasco on his ass this round, the crowd will have to decide the winner, because I'm not letting this continue. You'd better do something, Malcolm. Don't let this spiral any further out of control. If you lose to him…"

"Stop making me tell you to shut up, Nash," I snarl.

"Round three it is then!" Nash calls out to everyone as he blows the horn once again.

Red-faced and furious, Fiasco runs towards my side of the cage, his right hand cocked for the same opening haymaker he threw the last two rounds. I was ready last time and thought that taking the fight to his body would wear him down. I was wrong. His midsection is, if possible, even harder than his thick skull. There's nothing I can hit him with that is going to put him down before he manages to get in a shot that turns off my lights.

Unless…when I duck under his punch, his fist crashes into the gate, the bone in his dislocated pinky finger shifting as it slams into the metal. In the last two rounds, he had spun back to me so quickly I couldn't retaliate; but this time he visibly cringes and hesitates a moment, his right arm dropping as a spasm of pain rips through him.

I don't waste my chance. Fiasco is a few inches taller than I am, so when I leap onto him and wrap my arms around his neck, I know I must look ridiculous, like a child getting a piggy-back ride from his father. I try to jerk his head back to get my forearm across his windpipe; but as soon as Fiasco feels me climbing him, he drops his head forward, tucking his chin and protecting himself.

I grab his face and throw my weight backwards, trying to shift this concrete-smashing giant off balance and take him to the ground. That completely fails as Fiasco simply spins around slightly bent forward, and then begins slamming his back into the cage trying to shake me off. I keep one arm pressuring his chin, trying to force it upward, while with the other I hammer heavy punches into the side of his face.

With an uncharacteristic high-pitched screech, Fiasco abruptly surges forward away from the cage wall, leaps into the air with me still clinging to his back, and spins around to crash down onto the wooden floor of the cage. When his body weight slams down on me, I almost lose my grip; but when he begins speaking, my fury redoubles and I feel my strength returning.

"You want to fight like a cheap little-bitch?" Fiasco huffs as he squirms on top of me. He begins trying to throw his elbows back into my stomach, but he's so wide compared to me that he can only graze me. "I'm going to pound you into this floor, then I'm going to go pound Naomi into your bed. You hear me, Malcolm? I love you, prez, but I'm going to put you down!"

I force my arm over his mouth and chin, which he is still tucking down as hard as his iron-neck muscles will allow. "You will never touch Naomi," I hiss into his ear. "You will never look at Naomi," I continue, as I use my free hand to punch him in the eye. "You're never even going to *smell* Naomi," I roar.

"Goddamned dirty mother...." Fiasco manages to choke out as I jam my forearm across his neck. As soon as my arm is in position, I use my free hand to lock my grip across his neck.

Fiasco bucks and thrashes on top of me like a shark hauled out of the ocean. I take a deep breath and hold on for all I am worth, knowing that if he breaks free, and if the crowd judges this fight...I'm going to lose. My only chance is to put my old friend down for a nap. And unless I can knock him unconscious, he *will* take Naomi away.

"You...won't...have...her!" I roar as the thought sends a final surge of strength through my body. Fiasco's thrashing slows, but my words must inspire something within him as well, because he suddenly rolls to his side and begins forcing himself up onto his hands and knees while I'm still clinging onto him, throwing all my weight into strangling him.

My face is pressed into Fiasco's shoulder, and I can see that his face has turned an inhuman shade of purple, his tongue actually gagging out of his wide-open mouth. I can also see him curl his huge fist up, and I have no defense as it rises once more towards my uncovered face, attempting to hammer me off of his back. I close my eyes to brace myself for the impact.

CHAPTER FOURTEEN

Naomi

As soon as I hear the rumble of Malcolm's bike, I roll over in his bed and put my back to the door, pretending to be asleep.

I started to go home to sleep in my own bed, but the truth was, I wanted to know who won tonight. Besides, Malcolm and I made a deal, one I plan to keep. I'm trying really hard to trust him, even if he is a dick for putting me in this position.

True, I guess it's my own fault for putting myself in this position, stealing from my father and getting caught stealing from the MC to pay him back.

I hear the front door open and close, then the sound of heavy footsteps growing louder on the hardwood floor as he stomps toward the bedroom. His feet stop abruptly before resuming their course toward the bed.

"Wake up, honey," Malcolm's gruff voice says in the darkness before he turns a lamp on. "Time to go to Fiasco's..."

"What?" I exclaim when I shoot straight up in bed to look at him. "You lost?"

"Of course not," he says as he removes his jeans, his shirt already missing. And in the glow of the light, I can see cuts and bruises scattered over his flesh and his face...wow, his handsome face has seen better days. Despite the swelling, his lips are lifted in a grin. He peels the covers back and then lies down in his bed beside me naked. "I choked the shit out of that big bastard and forced him to tap out. Now, how about you climb on top of me and ride my dick to thank me for winning. Let's see if you can make me tap out on that ass."

A scoff leaves my lips. "Go fuck yourself, Malcolm."

When I lay my head back down on the pillow, I roll to my side away from him.

"Come on, honey, don't be that way," he says with his rough, smoker's chuckle. Moving toward me underneath the covers, he presses the front of his body to my backside. Then, he not so subtly reaches around to slide his fingers down into the front of my panties that I'm wearing with just one of his t-shirts.

"I was never going to lose," he says. "I just needed to let off a little steam, put the fucker in his place. Fiasco's a decent fighter, just not as good as I am."

If his words are supposed to make me feel better, they don't. Now it sounds like he offered me up in a fight just for shits and giggles.

Malcolm lowers my panties in the back, and then I feel his dick poking me in my ass cheeks, right down the center of my crease. He rubs his hard shaft through my damp folds, my body turned on even if I'm still pissed at him.

"You didn't miss me today?" he asks.

"No."

"Not even a little?" On the word *little*, he eases his blunt head inside of my cunt and pulls it right back out.

"No," I lie as I grab a fistful of sheets.

"Well, I missed you and this pussy," Malcolm tells me, his lips finding the skin around the opening of my shirt collar. "Every time my fist landed, it was for this pussy." He eases his dick inside again and retreats. "And for these tits." Malcolm reaches around and squeezes a handful, making my entrance weep even more for him, allowing him to enter her a few more inches. Malcolm's deep masculine grunt of pleasure against my ear sends a wave of heat through my body, turning my limbs to liquid.

"That's it. Just relax and let me have you. I promise it'll feel good," he whispers. "You know you want it."

With another scoff at his arrogance, I try to squirm away from him, but Malcolm doesn't let me. He rolls me over, pinning my back to the mattress, his face hovering right above mine.

"What's the problem, honey? I felt how much you want me, so why the hell are you playing hard to get?"

"I'm mad at you, Malcolm! What you did...it was *really* fucked up. You treated me like-like I'm an object you can just throw away!"

"I'm sorry," he says, looking pretty pitiful and sincere thanks to the darkening bruise around his eye. "From your point of view, I guess what I did looks bad, but there was *never* a chance I wouldn't win. I knew that, or I wouldn't have challenged him in the first fucking place. And just so you know, the alternative to fighting him was to have him bring a vote to the table that they should *all* get to have a turn with you since you stole from the entire club. That wasn't going to fucking happen, so I had to give him something to shut him up."

"You could've at least talked to me about it first!" Since there's enough room between us for me to roll over again, I do it so that I don't have to look at the swelling in his face or his piercing green eyes that always seem to make my heart race and my body melt, even when I'm pissed at him.

"So that's how it's going to be? You're not going to talk to me or let me fuck you?" he asks. I don't respond since the answer should be pretty damn clear. "That's too bad. I bought you a little something before my fight. Don't you want to see it?"

"No."

The mattress shifts, and then I hear Malcolm rustling around me, the jingling sound making me think he's digging through his jeans. A moment later, the mattress dips again from his added weight and he dangles something in front of my face – a silver necklace that he then fastens at the back.

Curious to see what small token he thinks is actually going to soothe my anger, I reach down to pick up whatever is weighing the chain down in the front. It's a clear floating locket full of charms surrounded by black and yellow gemstones, the same colors as his bike. Well, I assume they're fake gemstones and not actually diamonds because that would be ridiculous. There's also a tiny boat charm, an ace of spades playing card, and a skull head like the one on Malcolm's jacket.

"It's beautiful," I say aloud because I love it, not for whatever its monetary value may be, but because of the thought he put into it – giving me little pieces of himself.

While I'm still admiring his peace offering, Malcolm starts placing open-mouthed kisses on my hip bone, his facial hair coarse as it brushes against my skin, contrasting with his smooth, damp lips and tongue.

When he finally presses on my hips to flatten them on the bed, I don't resist. Crawling over between my thighs, he spreads them wide enough for his broad shoulders to wedge underneath. With a single finger, he tugs the crotch of my panties to the side, and then his mouth...god, his filthy, filthy mouth, gently kisses and licks along the seam of my pussy lips.

Teasing me, that's what he's doing.

His fingertip slides through my slit before the tip of his tongue follows the same path. His long hair is still damp from his recent shower that he must have taken at the clubhouse. The strands graze lightly over my skin with every little move he makes.

"Malcolm," I moan as he keeps up the tickling sensation, up and down, up and down until I'm panting and grabbing two handfuls of his wet hair to pull his mouth closer to where I need it. Eventually, on his own schedule, his tongue moves up and licks rapid little circles right over my swollen bundle of nerves.

"Uh! Uh! *Uh god!*" I cry out. My hips rock forward and back toward his mouth. The pleasurable warmth builds in my lower belly until I feel like I'm going to burst wide open. "Malcolm!" I scream as the dam inside of me splinters apart into a million pieces, unable to hold back the waves of ecstasy. I ride each and every one of them with my hips bucking and my back arching up off the mattress. At one point, Malcolm even has to slap his arm over my lower belly to hold me down so he can keep tormenting me in the best way possible with his tongue. The sight of the dark tattoos along his forearm and his muscular bicep that's flexing while his bearded face is pressed between my legs is so damn hot. A girl could get used to this sort of treatment, even if he sometimes acts like a dick.

Only after the waves of pleasure crest and crash a second time does Malcolm's mouth finally relent.

His long, hard shaft slams inside of me before I know he's even moved up the bed. Then, his mouth is crashing down on my panting one, shoving his tongue inside, making me taste myself.

"Oh fuck, Naomi," Malcolm pulls back suddenly to groan against my lips. Grabbing my thighs, he says, "Knees up to your chest, honey. I need to be deeper."

I do as he asks, my hands gripping my knees that are near my shoulders. When he rams into me hard and fast on the next thrust, I scream in part pleasure and part pain, worried he might tear me in half.

Somehow, despite the position of my raised knees, our mouths meet again, frantic for each other as he fervently moves in and out of me. Malcolm is eventually the first one who pulls away again, both of us panting.

"I wish I could stay buried...right fucking here...forever," he grunts as he stares down into my eyes, the rhythm of his thrusts faltering. "But fuck, if I'm not already close after needing you all day long."

"Stay," I tell him, meaning he doesn't have to pull out. Letting go of my knees, I reach around to dig my fingers into his tight, flexing ass cheeks, keeping him deep.

He closes his eyes and groans before looking back down at my face. "You on the pill?"

"Uh-huh," I tell him with a nod and bite down on my bottom lip to try and hold off on coming until he's ready.

"You sure?" he asks again, jaw clenched tight.

"Yes."

I see the second his control snaps. Malcolm's face goes slack as his entire body sags above me, like the weight of the world has been lifted from his shoulders. His hips slam inside me one last time, and then his hot release coats my walls, filling me up with rapid bursts that send me crashing over the edge again.

∾

Malcolm

I HONESTLY DON'T KNOW what the fuck just happened, why I decided to trust Naomi, a woman who I know for a fact is a thief and a liar.

It sounds stupid even in my head, but there was just this moment when we were looking into each other's eyes and I saw her, really saw her, Naomi. All the little things that make her who she is on the inside was in them. It felt like I knew her, and she knew me like no one else before.

Tomorrow, I'll blame it on the endorphins and testosterone all mixing together from the fight, and then the fucking after Naomi finally forgave me for being a dick.

I shouldn't give a shit that she was pissed off, but I did; I have all fucking day. That's why I went and picked out the necklace for her, spending even more money than I should since I'm already down twenty thousand because of her.

As soon as I roll off of Naomi and flop onto the bed, she turns her face to look at me. Her fingertips brush lightly over the swelling and bruises that are probably more visible now than an hour ago. "Serves you right," she tells me.

"I haven't handled all this as well as I could have," I agree. "I told my boys tonight I made some mistakes, but I'm going to get it all straightened out. They're just going to have to understand that you and I are...well, we're something. I guess we don't have to figure out everything tonight. The important thing is that business with Fiasco is settled.

"Fiasco was never an important thing," Naomi mumbles as she snuggles down onto me. "Good night, Malcolm. Stop overthinking everything and just relax."

I lie there, stroking her hair, trying to do just that; and at some point, sleep sneaks up on me and puts me under the same way I did Fiasco a few hours ago.

CHAPTER FIFTEEN

Naomi

"Time to get up and get ready to leave," Malcolm tells me with a slap to my bare bottom that's hanging out of the covers before my eyes are even fully opened. Last night I slept like a dead woman in the deepest, best sleep of my life. What woman wouldn't have been comatose after so many amazing orgasms? Not to mention the relief that Malcolm won the fight. If he had lost, I wouldn't have gone along and been with Fiasco just because the two men agreed to the arrangement for me.

"Where are we going?" I ask, sitting up to stretch my arms over my head and work the kinks out of my neck.

"To settle up with Harry," Malcolm answers as he walks over to a dresser wearing nothing but a blue towel around his hips. Thanks to his dripping wet hair, his back is covered in water droplets from his shower. Guess he's been up for a while, but I can't believe I didn't notice him rattling around the small house. I'm still half-asleep and so distracted by the sight of him mostly naked that it takes a few seconds for his words to sink in.

"Harry? We're going to see him right now?"

"Yeah. You owe him money, right? It's time to pay up."

"And you're just going to walk up to him and hand him a stack of cash?" I ask.

"I said I would take care of him, and I will," he mutters. Dropping the towel, he steps into a pair of jeans and pulls them up sans underwear.

"Okay. Thanks," I tell him.

Flashing me a crooked grin, he says, "I know a better way for your mouth to thank me."

"Oh, so you're finally going to let me blow you?" I ask while my fingers play with the floating charm on my necklace, moving it back and forth on the chain.

"I have a mind to make you get on your knees and suck me off right the fuck in front of Harry," Malcolm tells me. "But we should probably wait until we get home before you pull my dick out, so he doesn't feel the need to put a bullet in me. At least no more so than usual."

"You scared of him?" I ask curiously.

"Fuck no," he mutters. "But I'm not stupid. My whole crew is going with us, and I won't turn my back on that snake for a second."

"Good," I reply. "He's an asshole who can't be trusted."

"Like father, like daughter?" he remarks.

"He's the one who put me up to stealing from you!" I remind him.

"After you stole from him. What did you use the money for?" he asks.

"What does it matter?" I ask.

"Just curious to know what you would risk your life for. If you weren't his kid, I have no doubt your body would be bloated and floating in the middle of the ocean somewhere."

"Thank you for that lovely image," I scoff.

"The truth is usually ugly, honey. You're old enough to have figured that out by now."

"Oh, I have," I assure him.

"Right, well get your ass up and get dressed. We're meeting the guys in half an hour."

"Okay. Good thing I grabbed a change of clothes from my place before work yesterday." I sigh heavily as I force myself out of the warm, comfy bed and make my way to the bathroom. A quick glance over my shoulder confirms that Malcolm's eyes are on my naked ass, watching it like it's a big ole jar of honey and he's a ravenous bear.

"Like what you see?" I tease him.

"I'd like it even better if it was doing what I fucking said," Malcolm remarks. "Get some clothes on before I have to fuck you over the sink, and you make us late."

"You're the president, remember?" I remind him while turning my back to the doorframe and cupping my breasts to fondle them suggestively. "You can be late if you want, and nobody could do a damn thing about it."

"I hate being late," he growls. "But I fucking hate walking around with a hard dick even more." Stomping over to me while jerking the zipper of his jeans down, he says, "Bend over the counter and spread your legs. I'll rub my cock on your clit until you get wet enough to take it."

"Yes, sir," I easily agree when he grabs me by the elbow and ushers me into the bathroom.

∼

Malcolm

I WOKE up this morning with my face and my dick throbbing so hard I gave up on sleep and took a hot shower to try and relieve both aches. Turns out that getting off inside Naomi is one helluva pain reliever, making me so relaxed that I don't think anything can get to me today, not even Harry fucking Cox. Silas was right — I did need a little stress relief in my life.

My new state of pussy-induced zen is the reason I decide to squash shit with Fiasco as soon as Naomi and I get to the clubhouse. The rest of the guys are standing around with their bikes in the parking lot, waiting for us.

"About fucking time," Fiasco mutters when my bike cuts off. He's standing the furthest away, his thick arms crossed over his chest, a pouty scowl on his face that's more notable thanks to his busted lip. He'd gotten hold of a tongue depressor and some duct tape to hold his busted finger in position. I rethink my decision to make amends with him when his eyes eat up Naomi in her tight, yellow cotton halter top and frayed denim shorts, which are so tiny that I've seen panties with more fabric. She's hot as hell, I know, but that doesn't mean I enjoy having a man she's been with before eye-fucking her like he's remembering every second of what she did with him.

But for now, she's mine, not Fiasco's or anyone else's. I made sure that argument, at least, is settled.

"Stay here," I tell Naomi, reaching back to give her a very intentional stroke of my palm up her bare, tan thigh before I climb off my bike and march up to him, my helmet still on in case he decides he didn't get to throw enough punches last night. I need to keep some of my brains unscrambled if I plan to stay in charge of the MC.

"We cool?" I ask Fiasco, holding out my palm to him. He stares down at it for several silent seconds, refusing to uncross his arms.

"You shouldn't have beat me. I had the upper hand the entire time," he grumbles.

"I know. I got lucky in the end," I say to try and smooth things over with my brother rather than rub the truth in his face – I'm a smarter, faster fighter than he is which is how I was able to force him to tap out. If anything, that's probably what pisses him off the most. He had no choice but to give up unless he wanted to be choked out.

Men like us don't enjoy quitting. We prefer to fight to the bitter end, no matter the cost. I embarrassed him by forcing the surrender, more so than if I had knocked his lights out with a hit.

"Whatever," Fiasco huffs. A moment later, he rolls his eyes, lowers his arms and shakes my hand.

I squeeze the bones in his hand harder than necessary before I lower my voice to warn him, "Do yourself a favor and don't forget our deal or try some bullshit with Naomi because your feelings got hurt. You don't talk to her or touch her; and if you want to keep your eyeballs in your head, you'll stop staring at her. Understand me?"

"Yeah, prez," he replies, sneaking only a brief glance over at Naomi, who has her head turned, looking over her shoulder at us. "I gotcha."

"Good," I tell him as I let his hand go. Speaking up so the rest of the guys can hear me, I say, "Let me do the talking today with this prick. Your job is to keep your eyes open and be ready to fuck things up if shit goes sideways."

"You sure about this, prez, walking into this asshole's palace?" Dev asks.

"Don't worry, I've got a plan, one that hopefully won't lead to a single drop of blood," I assure the guys. "Now let's go and get this over with."

When I stroll over and prepare to throw my leg over my bike, Naomi says, "Fiasco barely has a scratch on him."

Grinning, I tell her, "Yeah, well, the worst of his scars are on the inside – I broke his pride, but it'll heal eventually." Once I'm in position, I warn Naomi over my shoulder, "Better hold on tight, honey. After all the fucking trouble you've caused me, it wouldn't do to lose you on the side of the road somewhere."

Her arms wind around my waist and double up so that they're locked so tightly I can barely breathe when she rests the chin of her helmet on my back. "Something tells me that you enjoy a little bit of trouble, Malcolm."

"Amen to that," I chuckle before I crank the engine and take off.

～

"Remember, let me do all the talking," I whisper to Naomi as two of her dad's goons lead us inside the front of his three-story mansion after we park our bikes and remove our helmets. "You hear me, honey? This is a tricky situation, so I don't need you going and making it any worse."

"Yeah, I hear you," she sniffs indignantly, not liking the order, but hopefully knowing it's best to let me handle her old man.

"Who the...what the fuck is he doing here?" Harry demands from his throne, his round face turning blood red when my crew and I walk into his house like we own it with Naomi by my side. "What are you doing here, Malcolm?" he grits out, sitting up a little straighter. "And who kicked your ass? I'd like to send them a thank you card."

"Is that how you're really going to play this?" I scoff, ignoring his attempt at a joke. "You know why I'm here. Did you think I wouldn't figure out that you sent your goddamn daughter to fucking rob us?"

Harry's throat works as he swallows hard around that piece of information as his eyes narrow at Naomi, already thinking of ways to make her pay for screwing him over and putting him in this position. Fuck if I'll let that happen.

"Naomi's a grown woman," he says. "She goes and does whatever the hell she wants. I can't and won't take responsibility for her. Hell, did she tell you she stole from me too?"

"Liar," I retort. Normally I would've yelled and called him every name in the book by now, but again, I'm chill as fuck thanks to emptying my balls in his daughter.

Still, despite my calm, my fists clench in anger by my sides when he says, "That's a rich accusation coming from the son of a bitch who fucked my woman behind my back."

"Actually, I never touched Delilah. I just made her end things with you to prove a point – that she was a traitorous gold-digging bitch who would get on her knees for whoever she thought was her next big pay day."

"You should've minded your own goddamn business and stayed out of mine," he grits out.

"I came here to tell you the same fucking thing, old man, and to see if you're still holding a grudge. It's been over two years. You need to get the fuck over it.," I reply. Of course this dumb bastard is going to try and act all innocent, not giving a shit if his mess blows back entirely on Naomi. "It's a shame you can't get your head out of your ass. I had a damn good offer to settle up whatever debt Naomi owes you," I inform him.

"Why the hell would you do that?" Harry asks. Some of the red tint fades to white in his wrinkled face. "Wait a second. Are you fucking her? You are, aren't you? You piece of shit!"

"Damn right I'm fucking her. Earning every single penny of the ten thousand I agreed to settle up with you," I tell him, which has Naomi calling me a few choice names under her breath.

"Why am I even surprised?" Harry asks. "For a man who hates gold-diggers, you're messing with the wrong girl, Malcolm. She's a whore just like her mother, fucking anything and everything for a dollar."

"You son of a bitch!" Naomi shouts at him, unable to keep her mouth shut another second after that cruel insult. "Don't you dare say shit about her!" She lunges for her father before I sling my arm around her waist to drag her backside flush with the front of my body. My dick, of course, reacts involuntarily, having gotten so attached to her ass the last few days and the amazing way it feels when she's molded to my crotch. Naomi notices my body's response to her and gasps before thankfully going still.

"Do you want me to pay up the ten she still owes you or not?" I ask Harry around her shoulder.

"She did owe me ten," Harry sniffs. "Now it's fifteen. She hasn't made any payments this week."

Asshole. I knew this was the game he would play, always

demanding more money because of his made-up, insanely high interest rates.

"Fine," I say with an annoyed sigh. "I've got a custom-built vintage hardtail chopper bike in the shop that's worth twenty K easy. It's yours if we can call it even?"

Craning her neck around to look at me, Naomi's blue eyes are wide in shock when she asks, "Why? Why would you give this bastard something worth way more than I owe him?"

"Because this greedy old bitch always demands more than the bottom line he thinks is due to him," I explain quietly to her. "And he can't resist a sweet deal for something that's one-of-a-kind."

"I too am confused as to why you're going above and beyond to pay off her debt," Harry says. "What's your angle here, Hyde?"

Naomi is going to hate me in a few seconds. Which is a shame since we just had make-up sex for our last fallout less than twelve hours ago. Still, the MC's best interest always comes first no matter what. The guys are my family. We're closer than blood, and we do anything for each other through the good times and the bad. Fiasco just happens to enjoy playing the part of the little brother who frequently causes problems for the rest of us.

"We hear you've recently grown your amphetamine business," I say to Harry.

"Malcolm!" Naomi exclaims, and I slap my palm over her mouth to keep her quiet.

"Well?" I ask Harry.

"What about my amphetamine business?" Harry asks.

"The Aces are looking to expand charters throughout the state, around big cities and universities. It would be an easy way for you to move product."

"You think we could be business partners?" Harry chuckles. "You're out of your damn mind, Hyde!"

Negotiating with this dickhead while Naomi fights my hold on her waist and mouth isn't easy by any means, but I can work with it.

"Suit yourself. Your loss, old man," I tell him. "We'd be willing to do a sixty-forty split your way, but I hear the Savage Kings of Myrtle Beach are offering a fifty-fifty deal..."

"Bullshit!" Harry exclaims. "I'm the only one dealing speed in the Carolinas!"

"Apparently not. And as big as the Kings are, they'll not only take over your business but shut you down with their ties to the feds by the end of the year."

"How many charters are you talking about expanding?" he asks, already coming around to the idea.

"At least five within a few months, maybe double that in a year's time. All near big colleges. You know how the co-eds depend on speed to get through exams..."

"Five, you say? How much product could you move at a time?"

"However much will fit in about twenty-five backpacks," I tell him honestly since that would be the mode of transportation. One on each biker's back, zipping down the highway, praying the police can't catch us.

"How often?" he asks now while rubbing his double chin in thought, now seriously considering the idea he thought was absurd a few seconds ago. That's how fuckers like him are all programed. He's no better than the gold-diggers we both hate since he's all about chasing dollar bills too.

"Once a month at first to see how it goes. But who knows? If things work out, maybe twice a month or as often as once a week."

That has his blond brow lifting with interest.

"I'll think about it," Harry says, even though we both know he's a greedy fuck who is going to say yes. "Get me the custom bike, and I'll be in touch."

"Sure thing," I tell him before I pick up Naomi and urge her forward, following my guys out the door who held up their ends of being silent but deadly threats. I'm glad it didn't come to that. I'd hate for any one of my boys to die because of a diseased old prick like Harry.

As soon as we're outside and I let my hold on her go, Naomi spins around and starts yelling at me. "I can't believe you! Why did you do that?" she screeches as my guys freeze mid-stride to stare. They've never heard anyone talk to me the way she is right now.

"Which part?" I ask just to be a jerk.

"You know which part!" Naomi exclaims, putting her palms on my chest and trying to shove me. She actually succeeds in sliding herself backwards a few inches, so she must have given it everything she had in her small frame.

"Calm the fuck down and get your ass on the bike," I order her quietly, offering her the spare helmet in my hand. But of course, she doesn't move. "We'll talk back at home," I assure her through clenched teeth.

"Fine," she huffs. "But only because we have a deal and I don't break my promises. If not for that, I wouldn't be able to look at your stupid face again!"

Her words have me biting back a grin as she jerks the helmet out of my hands and slams it down on her head, nearly busting her nose in anger.

Yep, I'm definitely gonna have to do some serious ass kissing if I want her back in my bed tonight.

CHAPTER SIXTEEN

Naomi

I'm surprised smoke isn't coming out of my ears and nose. I'm so angry!

How could Malcolm agree to a business deal with that sleazy, old man! I thought he was on my side, not that asshole's!

"Yo, Dev!" Malcolm calls out as soon as he turns his bike off in front of their clubhouse. "Mind grabbing my chopper and taking it back on the trailer?" He pulls out some keys from his pocket and dangles them from his fingers.

"Are you sure about this?" Devlin asks, echoing my sentiments. "You've been working on this bike forever."

"Malcolm, you don't have to do this!" I tell him when I grab the front of his leather cut.

"Yeah, I do," he says. "Cash isn't going to be enough for a greedy asshole like Harry. He'll keep upping the price, coming back for more until you give him what he *thinks* is his fair share. That's how those mafia motherfuckers do business." Then, narrowing his dark green eyes as he glares at me and his friend, he says, "And I've about reached my goddamn tolerance limit on having all of my fucking decisions second-guessed today!"

"I *never* asked you do to this," I remind him.

"I told you I would take care of your debt with Harry, and that's what I'm doing," he tells me. Turning to the other man, he throws the keys in his direction so that he has no choice but to take them. "Go get the damn bike, Dev."

"If you're sure..." Devlin mutters.

"Congratufuckinglations. You're taking my shift on the boat tonight too," Malcolm says. The man backs away cursing, but then he gets back on his bike and rides away without any further protests.

"I don't like this," I tell Malcolm. "You giving up your bike and going into business with him. Is that...is that what this has been about the whole time? You were using me to get to Harry?" I ask in concern, more hurt than pissed at the moment as those ideas begin to suffocate me.

"No, the idea just came to me last night," he answers. "The guys want to grow, and what better way than with a new drug?"

"Selling drugs is wrong, Malcolm."

"Hey, we don't make anyone take them," he huffs defensively as he lights up a cigarette, like the slave he is to his nicotine addiction. "If they don't buy from us, they'll buy from someone else, so what the fuck does it matter?"

"It's illegal!" I yell at him.

"Are you blind? So is about ninety percent of everything else we do," he chuckles around the cancer stick hanging out of his lips. "Don't worry about me, honey. I'm not getting locked up anytime soon."

"How do you know that?" I ask. "Harry could set you up!"

"He's not that stupid. The man loves money more than he wants revenge, especially since he now knows I never touched his ol' lady."

"Was that even true?" I ask softly.

"Yes, it was true! Do you really think I would ever fuck someone who had been with Harry?"

"No, but..."

"But nothing," Malcolm says when he grabs either side of my shoulders and speaks around his cigarette in my face. "And I've heard enough of your mouth for the day. You can't question me and yell at me in front of my own fucking MC, Naomi!"

"Sorry," I mutter. I know he's super pissed at me and that he's sacrificing something important to him to help me. That custom bike he built must have taken months or even years, and he's just giving it away to help me get out from underneath Harry, going above and beyond so that the asshole won't keep coming back and asking for more money. "Thank you," I add since I haven't said that yet.

"I'm not doing it out of the goodness of my heart, honey," he chuckles as he removes the smoke from his mouth. Grabbing my necklace in his other hand, he pulls me forward to shove his tongue into my parted lips for a dirty kiss that tastes like nicotine, a combination of black pepper and Malcolm, which I've quickly become addicted to.

"Right," I reply around his mouth. "You're only doing it out of the goodness of your dick."

On the next swipe of his tongue, I suck on it until Malcolm groans and pulls away.

"Did I mention I have an office inside the clubhouse too?" he asks, dropping his cigarette and stomping it out with his boot without letting go of my necklace.

"No, I don't believe you did," I answer. "I've only ever seen the bar and one of the storage rooms..."

As soon as Malcolm's fingers abruptly drop my necklace and he takes a step backward, I realize the mistake I've made – mentioning the place I fooled around with Fiasco.

"Just wait here while I go handle some shit inside," he says when he turns and starts toward the building.

"Malcolm, hold on! I'm sorry. Please show me your office!" I call out to him. He holds up his palm for me to stop, clearly signaling that he's heard enough.

∼

Malcolm

I'M TURNING INTO A PUSSY.

That's the only explanation there is for why I give two shits about who Naomi's been with before me. I know full well about what she did with Fiasco, and yet every time I'm reminded of it, it's like getting hit with a sledgehammer to the guts. The feeling isn't getting better with time either. If anything, it's intensifying. My jealousy is growing worse every second of the day that I'm with Naomi, and I have no idea how to stop it. The emotion defies logic and common sense, causing me to lash out and hit things – like the door to the chapel that now has a fist-shaped dent in it.

And hell, I can't even remember why I had to come inside the pool hall in the first place. I'm pretty sure it was just my knee-jerk reaction to the jealousy that overwhelmed me. I had to walk away before I did something insane, like drag Naomi up on the roof to fuck her in front of the world in an attempt to appease my alpha tendencies.

After I sit my ass down in my chair at the head of the Dirty Aces' meeting table and smoke half a pack of cigarettes, I finally feel calm enough to face her again. Surprisingly, the woman is still in the same place I left her and straddling my bike with her helmet on.

"Ready?" she asks with a hesitant smile like she's unsure of my mood.

"Yeah."

"Would you mind taking me by my house to grab a few more

things?" she asks while reaching inside her helmet to push her short hair out of her eyes, looking sweet and innocent when we both know the truth.

"Fine," I agree when I climb on in front of her.

After I crank the bike up, Naomi wraps her arms around my waist and shouts, "Do you need directions?"

"Nope," I respond before I take off.

Rushing past the world at a high rate of speed is just as cathartic as usual. In fact, I've reeled in my anger by the time we park outside the white, rundown farmhouse, leaving only the simmering jealousy.

"This place looks like it would fall over if I sneeze on it," I tell Naomi after we both dismount and remove our helmets.

"It's not that bad," she scoffs before leading the way up the steppingstones to the front door. I don't even know why I'm surprised when she pulls a key free from underneath a flowerpot with some unknown plant that's wilted in the dry summer heat.

"Nice security system you've got there," I tell her rather than lecture her about how dangerous leaving a key on the porch like that could be.

"Nobody ever comes out this way," she says when she pushes the door open and walks inside. "I'll grab some things from upstairs and be right back."

Once she's gone up the creaking stairs, I stroll around through the living room where the dusty furniture looks like it's several decades old. There are several colorful, handmade quilts tossed around and a thick old-school television that I'm surprised still works. Above the fireplace that probably hasn't been used in years because of the heat the coast endures all year lately, there are several framed photos of a man and a woman, their wedding photo and then one where both of their hair has turned grey. Then, there's a school picture of a young woman, who looks similar to Naomi, before a picture of a toddler, who I have no doubt is the woman upstairs. The kid has her big, blue eyes and light blonde hair, looking like a tiny angel with a sweet, innocent grin on her face that probably got her out of any trouble she caused.

Even years later, she still has that same power over me despite how much I fucking hate it.

I hear her footsteps on the squeaky stairs before I hear her voice. "All set. Let me just grab a bag."

She walks by me with a folded stack of clothes and a small plastic container on top.

"What's that?" I ask her when she grabs a plastic grocery bag from somewhere and stuffs her things into it.

"This?" she asks, holding up the piece of plastic.

"Yeah."

"Birth control," she answers with a grin that sends my mind right into the gutter as I immediately think about taking her again tonight without a rubber getting in the way.

Apparently reading my mind, Naomi sets her bag down on a brown leather chair and walks right up to me. She grabs my belt buckle to undo it as she sinks down to the floor on her knees.

And for the second time in a week, I find myself turning down a chance to fuck her sweet mouth.

"What are you doing?" I ask.

"What does it look like?" she replies as my belt comes free of the buckle.

"No," I say, grabbing her hands to still them before she can pull out my dick and I change my mind.

"No?" she repeats, blue eyes widening in surprise and what looks like disappointment that I'm rejecting her again.

"No," I reiterate. Clearing my throat when I turn away from her to fix my belt, I ask, "Do you need anything else?" I need to change the subject, because for the life of me I don't have any answers to what the hell my problem is, and I'm sure she's about to ask.

"No."

"Good. It's hot as hell in here, and I'm ready to get home," I tell her.

"Oh, sorry," she says as she gets to her feet again. "The, um, air conditioner is broken, and I haven't had a chance to fix it."

"Good thing you don't have to stay here tonight, isn't it?"

"Yeah," she agrees with a sigh, shoving her clothes into a plastic bag. "Good thing."

CHAPTER SEVENTEEN

Naomi

Malcolm is so icy that it's freaking me out. In fact, after we get back to his house, he doesn't come straight to bed. I take a long shower, hoping he'll join me. He doesn't. So, after I dry my hair, I sit down on the bed and wait...

He turned down another blowjob from me, which would be a first for any other man, but is the second time for Malcolm. Now, I'm afraid to try and make a move for fear of him rejecting me yet again.

I don't like the way it feels when he *doesn't* want me. My entire body is off-kilter, like I can't remember how to sit still or stand up straight. I'm anxious and annoyed.

After eleven, I give up and climb under the covers. Of course, with my mind in so much turmoil, I can't sleep. I just lie there, waiting for him.

When Malcolm does finally come into the bedroom minutes or

hours later, I hold my breath to see what he'll do, hoping — hell, *praying* — that he'll touch me.

But he doesn't. His weight shifts the mattress in the dark, and then...nothing.

I wait and wait, hearing his heavy exhales in the dark before I finally cave. Rolling over to his side of the bed, I throw my arm around his naked waist as I spoon him from behind. Like the other nights, at least he's still sleeping in the nude and didn't feel the need to come to bed in jeans to add a barrier between us.

"What the fuck are you doing?" he asks gruffly.

"Cuddling."

"I don't cuddle."

"Okay," I reply, but I don't move an inch.

"Naomi?"

"Yes?" I ask, my chin resting on his shoulder.

"Give me some space."

"No."

"What did you say?" he asks.

"I said no, I'm not going to give you space. You're angry at me and maybe pissed about losing your custom bike, and so I'm going to cuddle you until you fall asleep. Hopefully tomorrow you'll wake up and want to touch me again."

Malcolm's quiet for several long minutes, so long I think he's not going to say another word. Then, I hear a mumbled, "I don't share."

"You don't share?" I repeat.

"That's right."

"Okay."

"I hate that he had you first," he explains, the *he* obviously referring to Fiasco. And I can't help but grin to myself, because this big, bad ass man sounds like a pouting child who had to share his favorite toy. That's me. At the moment, I'm his favorite toy, which is incredibly wrong but still makes me feel invincible.

"You had me best," I tell him to try and appease his ego.

"Damn right," he mutters.

Does Malcolm think I still want Fiasco? If so, he's crazy not to see just how hard I'm falling for him.

CHAPTER EIGHTEEN

Malcolm

The next morning, I'm sitting in the chair at the head of the Dirty Aces' meeting table bright and early, waiting on the rest of the crew to roll into the clubhouse. I sent them a text late last night letting them know to be here early, before any of them had to get to their day jobs. Since it's an unusual meeting time, I brought some biscuits and have a pot of coffee and aspirin on standby for any hangovers that show up.

Devlin, Silas, Wirth, and Nash all show up together, which only leaves Fiasco missing. I'm not particularly worried about him being late, as he often doesn't respond to text messages. I'm not one hundred percent convinced he can even read.

"Hated to call you all in this early," I begin once they are all seated, "but I need to make some calls today, and I wanted to speak with you about it together before I get this started. You guys all know we have been talking about opening up our membership a bit and getting some new blood into the crew, most likely by merging with some other clubs. Nash has been helping me narrow down some prospects, and we wanted to see what you guys thought about hosting the Knights of Wrath this weekend."

"The Knights?" Devlin asks. "Isn't that Robert Greene's crew out near Fayetteville?"

"What's left of them," Silas snorts. "I think there are only three or four that aren't in prison for the rest of their damned lives. Those were some dumb mother-fuckers for cooking heroin."

"The dumb ones all got arrested," Nash interjects. "What's left of Robert Greene's crew are the good ones, the ones that might make good Aces, if we decide we can get along with them."

"Did someone say Bobby G.?" Fiasco exclaims as he bursts into the chapel. "We thinking about getting Bobby G. and his guys out here to party with us? Those boys are wild; we have to do it!"

"Thanks for joining us and offering your opinion," Nash scowls.

"No trouble," Fiasco replies as he takes his seat. "Is that all this is about? Inviting those guys out for the weekend? Shit, in that case, thanks for the free biscuit!"

"Well, that's Fiasco's vote," I tell the table. "Silas, you don't sound too impressed. What do you say?"

"I vote no," Silas shrugs. "I didn't have a very high opinion of that crew before, and hearing Fiasco vouch for them sealed the deal for me."

"Fuck you, Maybelline," Fiasco grins as he throws his half-eaten biscuit at Silas, who manages to knock it to the table before it explodes all over him.

"Goddammit, Fiasco, I've told you it's not mascara. I've just got dark eyes!" Silas growls in reply.

"So you say," Wirth interrupts. "Maybe you were just born with it?" he adds, making all the guys chuckle.

"Fuck you, too," Silas sulks as he crosses his arms over his chest.

"Enough," I silence them with a wave of the old, unloaded revolver we use as a gavel at the table. "Wirth, what's your vote?"

"Tell them to come on over, I don't mind," Wirth replies. "I don't know the boys, so it won't hurt to meet them."

"Same for me," Devlin agrees. "I vote to at least host them and see how we get along."

"All right, since Nash and I brought it to the table, you know our votes. That settles it," I confirm as I drop the butt of the pistol onto the table before tossing it down. "I'll make the calls, and we'll plan to have them out here next Saturday night. I want all of you to plan on being on the boat that night, and don't hold anything back. Act like you always do, so we can see how they react to us. We'll take another vote afterwards and see if we feel like they're a good fit for a patch over."

As the rest of the crew stands up and files out the door, Nash lays a hand on my arm to stop me from leaving. "You follow that advice yourself, you hear me, Malcolm? Be our president and represent us well. No more of this bullshit like we've had with Fiasco, okay?"

"You telling me you don't want Naomi working that night or something?" I ask him.

"I'm not telling you shit, just pointing out that she has caused problems..." Nash stops mid-sentence when he sees my face darkening. "Rather, there have been some problems, when she's been around. Just something to keep in mind," he finishes lamely before letting me go.

I sit back down at the head of the table as Nash leaves, trying to decide which way to go. I know Naomi needs the money, and the weekends are always when we bring in the big bucks on the gambling cruise. Fuck, when it comes down to it, the MC needs the money too, and she's by far the hottest girl we've got working right now. I'd be a fool not to let her work next weekend, I finally decide. Really, what's the worst thing that could happen? She already worked two shifts nearly naked and put up with people who have to be worse than the Knights of Wrath. She'll be fine, and it will work out best for everyone, I'm almost sure of it.

Naomi

THE NEXT WEEK with Malcolm goes by in a whirlwind of laughter, quickie sex, drinking, hard-core fucking, partying with the MC, working on the boat and, on a couple of occasions, gentle intimacy that felt very close to…well, if not lovemaking, it was the closest a rough biker like Malcolm could come.

By the time Saturday night rolled around, I was thoroughly confused about what had started off as a very black and white transaction. Malcolm had gone from just using me whenever he felt the urge to taking me out to dinner with him, having real discussions about his plans for the club with me, and he had stopped cringing away when I burrowed in next to him at night.

I wasn't sure what was going on in his head right now, but I certainly knew what was going on in my panties. My pussy was sore. I mean, I felt like I had ridden bareback across the wild west kind of sore. My entire crotch and even my ass cheeks felt inflamed and sensitive from the constant pounding they've taken.

As I move through the tables on the gambling cruise Saturday night handing out drink orders, the ache becomes even more pronounced, and I realize I still can't wait for more. What Malcolm and I have been doing together is so amazing that even though I need a rest, my body is positively quivering in anticipation of our next encounter.

As I come to the table where several members of the Dirty Aces are seated with the three members of the Knights of Wrath they had invited out tonight, I force my thoughts away from Malcolm Hyde. Unfortunately, just thinking about the way he had manhandled me earlier in his office before we left the dock causes my nipples to become puffy and swollen, rubbing almost painfully against the satin of the black tube dress I'm wearing tonight. At Malcolm's insistence, I haven't been wearing a bra much lately, and the three members of the Knights are eyeing my chest with interest.

"You see something you like here, huh?" the oldest of them asks me, a craggy-faced, bearded man I guessed was in his forties.

I flash a glance at Malcolm, who is sitting on the other side of the table, but his face is completely expressionless as he looks at the cards in his hand.

"Nothing like that," I demur. "I was on deck a moment ago, and the breeze is a bit chilly tonight."

"That's all it is, eh?" The scraggly old pervert scratches at his cheek as he pulls a small wooden box out of the leather cut he's wearing. "Well, stay a moment after you pass around those drinks. I want to pick your brain about how you feel working for these fine gentlemen."

As he's speaking, he lays the small box he had produced on the table, lifting a clasp and opening it to reveal a black, powdery substance. Dipping a tiny spoon concealed inside the box into the powder, he lifts it to his nose and snorts it with a ripping, sinus-grating gurgle.

Before I can ask what the hell he's doing, Silas, who's sitting beside Malcolm, speaks up. "You still cooking that stuff up, Bobby? Thought you gave all that up after your...troubles."

"Bah, we don't cook it in bulk anymore," Bobby laments. "This is just for personal use only these days. Of course, we still have a little income coming in from it here and there. The way we grind it means you don't have to inject it, which brings in a surprising amount of what I call 'health-conscious consumers.'"

"So you are still cooking enough to sell?" Silas persists, before I see Malcolm gently elbow him in the ribs.

"Their business isn't our business," Malcolm says softly. "At least not yet. If we all decide to move forward with any sort of arrangement, we can all sit down another time and work out business dealings. Tonight is just about having a good time."

"I'll drink to that, Mr. President," Bobby says as he rubs at his nose and snorts, before lifting his glass of whiskey to his lips and finishing it off in one swallow.

There is a palpable tension at the table as Silas, Nash, and Malcolm all sit in silence while Bobby looks around after finishing his drink. The two guys he brought with him are both staring at their cards when one of them says quietly, "You gonna call the pot or fold, Bobby? You're holding up the game."

"Oh, well, hell, I am," Bobby sneers, before looking over at me still standing beside the table. "I know a fine pot when I see one, and I tell you, boys, I'm all in on this one!" Laughing, he reaches over and slaps his hand, each finger adorned in a different gaudy ring, on the back of my thigh. "My god, what an ass on this one!" he exclaims, running his hand up the back of my dress, over my bottom before I can even move or protest. His fingertips drag right up the crack of my ass!

I leap forward and bump the table, letting out a tiny, surprised squeak as the old biker's hand gropes me. Before I can get a handle on the situation and slap him away, bodies seem to blur into motion all around me.

Malcolm erupts from his chair first, slamming his knees into the table and sending drinks, cards, and chips flying everywhere. Silas and Nash both try to grab at his arms as he storms around the table, but he shakes off both of them without even sparing them a glance.

"Malcolm, don't!" Nash manages to yell as the two other Knights scoot their chairs back and I grab helplessly at the edge of the table, still pinned there by the hand grabbing hold of my ass. The pressure disappears almost instantly as Malcolm whips around the bottle of Jack Daniels he had been sipping from on his side of the table, shattering it over the old biker's head and sending him sprawling to the floor!

"Malcolm!" I exclaim as he follows Bobby down to the ground, straddling him and slamming both of his fists into his face, one right after another. "Malcolm, stop it!" I shout when I grab his elbow and pull it back. "Please!"

Finally, he pauses long enough to look over his shoulder at me, strands of his long hair falling in his furious eyes. "He needs to learn a fucking lesson about touching shit that's not his!"

"I think you've made that lesson very clear. He's asleep, so you can stop hitting him now." I keep pulling on Malcolm's arm until he finally gets to his feet. "It wasn't a big deal. He just caught me by surprise, and...oh shit, Malcolm!"

When I glance around, everyone in the entire casino is gawking at us. Most of the other MC guys look a little on edge, but Malcolm's brothers? Well, Nash and Silas look pissed off at me more so than Malcolm, and I didn't even do anything!

"Come on," I tell him as I start pulling him in the direction of his office, his boys following behind us.

"We've got this," Nash says with a nod of his head toward the bar.

"Are you sure?"

"Yes. Get back to work," he snaps.

"Hey, it wasn't my fault that prick grabbed my ass!"

A humph is his response before the three men disappear.

"Whoa," Ronnie whispers when she comes over. "I've never seen Malcolm lose his shit like that before, especially not on the freaking president of another MC."

"What? You said he shot someone once..."

"Yeah, that was different. He calmly removed his gun from his pants, cocked it and then pulled the trigger. Tonight? Well, he looked like a rabid dog, all fists and no thought."

"Some jerk grabbed my ass!" I tell her in case she missed that part.

"*That's* what set Malcolm off?" she asks as if it's ridiculous. "Crazy. I thought the fight with Fiasco was just a pissing contest, but maybe it was more..."

"More what?" I ask in confusion.

"He must actually care about you," Ronnie says. "You're his old woman."

"His *old* woman?" I seethe.

"It's not a bad thing. It means he's laying claim to you as his publicly so that everyone knows you're taken. You should be flattered. It's not like the Aces to settle down."

Settle down?

The words repeat in my head over and over.

Is Ronnie right? Does Malcolm feel the same way about me as I do for him?

In just two days, our two-week arrangement is going to end. I've been dreading it all week because I'm not ready to lose him.

And maybe that feeling is mutual.

∼

Malcolm

"What the hell were you thinking?" Nash asks as he paces in front of my desk. "Robert Greene is the goddamn president of the Knights of Wrath MC. There might not be many of them on the outside, but you better hope his crew doesn't retaliate like we would if someone beat the shit out of you!"

"He reached under Naomi's skirt and grabbed her ass!" I mutter, clenching and relaxing my fist, my knuckles burning and bleeding as I think back to the moment I saw that motherfucker's hand disappear under her dress. I was on the other side of the table, so all I could do was watch as Naomi startled in surprise that someone was touching her so intimately without her consent before her stunned face looked like she wanted to vomit. "No, he didn't just grab it. He fucking fondled it."

"So?" Nash says.

"So, I taught him a lesson about touching shit that doesn't belong to him!"

"Oh, so Naomi belongs to you now?"

"Maybe."

"I thought she was just paying off a debt she owes you," he mutters.

"Right. She is."

"Until when?" he asks.

"A few more days or whatever." I act like I don't know the exact date that our deal ends when it's all I've been thinking about lately, wondering what happens afterward.

"And then what?" Nash asks.

"What do you mean?" I ask.

"Then what happens? You gonna cut her loose?"

"I haven't thought things through that far."

"That girl is fucking with your head, man," Silas says. "You've never let pussy mess you up like this before. That's why you're the one in charge."

"I don't know what you're talking about."

"The cage fight with Fiasco?" Nash remarks. "Throwing punches at the president of another MC? Those are not things a cool, rational leader does."

"Are you saying I'm doing a shit job?"

"Yeah, we are. Because lately you've been off your game. We all voted on this expansion, but now the Knights are probably going to back out of the patch over. You're trying your fucking best to get in the way of what's best for the club," Nash says.

"I'm not doing anything on purpose. Hitting Bobby was a one-off," I tell him. "Besides, you saw him snorting that shit, and you heard him admit they're still producing weight. There was never going to be any merger with those back-wood hillbillies."

"Maybe not!" Nash exclaims. "But there are diplomatic ways to handle that shit! You're supposed to know that; that's why you're the goddamned president!"

"Fuck you," I tell him. "I'm the president of the Aces because none of the rest of you could be bothered."

"Malcolm, man, you need to lose the girl," Silas speaks up and says, which isn't at all surprising coming from the man who treats all women like they're single-use condoms. Every woman is disposable to him, only good for spreading their legs.

"He's right," Nash agrees. "You already know she's shady as hell. No pussy is worth losing your cash and your head over."

"What the fuck is that supposed to mean?" I snap at him.

"That girl is all about the money, man," Silas answers. "She's using you, setting you up to be her baby daddy and meal ticket for the next eighteen years. If you haven't figured that shit out yet, then you need to get your head checked, Prez."

No, I don't believe that. Naomi doesn't care about money. She was only stealing from the Aces to pay back Harry.

But she never has told me why she had to steal from him…

I thought I was getting to know Naomi, but all I've really learned the last two weeks are the sounds she makes when she's coming on my tongue or cock and that she can't seem to get enough.

Could it just be an act, and she's only pretending to love fucking me until I knock her up?

"She's on birth control," I say aloud.

"That's what they all say," Silas grumbles. "How do you know for sure, though?"

"I've checked the pill container she leaves in the bathroom and see them missing each and every day," I assure them.

When Silas and Nash both share a knowing look, I want to knock their teeth out. "What?" I exclaim.

"What if she's flushing them?" Nash asks.

"Fuck you!" I shout at him. "She's not flushing her pills. Who the hell would do that?"

"Gold-diggers," Silas answers without missing a beat. "One of the oldest tricks in the books."

"Get the fuck out of my office!" I yell at the two of them and nearly lose my shit when they exchange a glance again. "You're wrong, and I don't want to hear another fucking word about her!"

"If you say so, prez," Silas mutters before they walk out and slam the door behind them.

∼

Naomi

MALCOLM DOESN'T SAY a word to me the rest of the night on the boat, or before he drives us home on his bike. The tension between us is back, the sensation exactly the same as when he was jealous of Fiasco and blaming it on me.

As soon as we walk through the door of his house, Malcolm snaps.

One minute I'm wondering if he's going to ever speak to me again for something that wasn't my fault; and then the next, he's slamming my back against the front door and pushing me down to my knees.

"Do you have any idea what you do to me?" Malcolm grits out softly when I'm kneeling on the floor.

"N-no," I answer in a whisper.

"Tonight I nearly killed a man," he goes on to say but I'm mostly distracted by his hands that are undoing his belt, popping the button on his jeans and lowering his zipper. "I nearly killed a man just for touching you."

I'm not sure how I'm supposed to respond to that information. I didn't like seeing Malcolm so out of control, but I can't lie. I do enjoy seeing his jealousy because it means he cares.

"You make me fucking crazy," he tells me as he pulls out his thick, semi-hard cock and gives it a few strokes, making it grow longer and causing my mouth to water for a taste. "I don't know if I'll ever be able to fuck your mouth without thinking about you getting on your goddamn knees for Fiasco in our stock room, sucking him off so good he was willing to fight me for you."

"It-it was just once," I remind him, unsure what else he wants me to say or why he's bringing that up now. "I barely remember it."

"Just one time, and he was ready to *fight* me for you," Malcolm reiterates. "If being addicted to your pussy is enough to have me ready to kill a man, I'm not sure if I can handle your mouth."

"I bet you can," I look up at his face to tell him before my gaze goes back to his hard length. "I really want to try."

"Take your dress off," he orders me, refusing to give me his decision on the matter just yet.

Reaching around to my side without breaking eye contact with Malcolm's dick, I find the zipper with my fingers and lower it. I shrug out of the material until it's completely off, leaving me in nothing but a bright yellow thong, one the same color as Malcolm's bike. I thought he might like the color on me. And judging by the way he steps back and tilts his head to the side to get a better look as his hand speeds up the movements on his dick, I think he does.

"So fucking beautiful," he says, but it doesn't sound like a compliment. It sounds like a complaint. Stepping forward again, he grabs my chin with his free hand and tells me, "Open your mouth wide."

My jaw falls open on command, stretching as wide as it can possibly go for him. Malcolm feeds the fat crown of his cock inside, rubbing his flesh along the flat of my wet tongue before pulling it back on a groan. He lets go of my chin to slap his palm to the door above my head and then pistons his cock in and out of my stretched mouth several quick times in a row. When his head hits the back of my throat, I gag and my mouth closes around his shaft instinctively, not biting but sucking him down deeper. My hands tear his jeans down his hips a little further so I can cup his balls.

"Jesus fucking Christ!" Malcolm roars with a hard slap of his palm on the door that startles a moan from me. "Please, Naomi," he begs, the only time I've ever heard him beg when he lets go of the base of his cock to grab the back of my head and hold it still. He shoves himself deeper into my mouth before retreating slowly with me sucking him so hard he grunts in pleasure. That's when his control snaps.

Malcolm's hips take over, and then he's using my mouth however the hell he wants, and there's nothing I would change. Tears run down my cheeks and mix with the drool from my mouth when Malcolm pins the back of my head to the door. I have no choice but to accept what he forcefully gives me of himself. At one point, he freezes with my nose pressed to his fuzzy pelvis and nowhere to go. Looking up at him as I hold my breath, I meet Malcolm's green eyes that are so heavy-lidded and dark they almost look black. His balls I'm still playing with are now pulled up tight to his body, telling me he's not going to last much longer.

"Swallow," he instructs me, and I follow his command. I would do anything this man asked me to do. "Again. Again. Ah-ah-*again*..." he trails off right before his entire body jerks and I taste his thick seed running down the back of my full throat. Once more his hips begin to buck furiously as he shouts my name like a curse and bangs his fist against the door. When I glance up, he's watching me as he rambles like I've never heard him do before.

"Oh fuck. Oh fuck me, that's so good, honey. Take it all, every drop. All your fault for draining me dry." He curses some more and then asks, "Are you wet?"

"Mmm-mm," I agree with a nod without taking my mouth off of him.

"Yeah? Show me. Fingers in your panties. Now, honey!" he demands when I take my time. "Rub that tight little pussy until I can remind it who it belongs to."

I finally get my fingers down into the fabric, and they sink right inside I'm so turned on, making me moan around Malcolm's girth.

"Your sexy mouth stays on my dick until you come, you hear me?"

I nod and hum my agreement, making his cock twitch before I pull my damp fingers out to tease my swollen clit.

"That feel good?" he asks as he keeps thrusting slowly, lazily in and out of my mouth, and I answer in the affirmative even though he already knows it does. I just think he loves the humming. "Better than my hand?"

I hum again and he grins down at me, causing butterflies to flutter around my belly. "Liar. If it were my fingers in your panties, you would've soaked through them by now. Hurry up and get yourself off so I can lick you clean."

The mention of his tongue between my legs causes my pussy walls to clench. God, he's so good at licking pussy that it should be illegal.

"That's right," Malcolm says, urging me on, knowing I'm getting close as he rolls his hips to keep his dick nice and hard in my warm, wet mouth. "I'm gonna handcuff you to my bed again so I can eat that pussy all night long. Your legs will shake so many times you won't be able to stand on them tomorrow."

I was doing good, right on the edge until he said the last word – tomorrow. Tomorrow's our last night together.

Reaching down to lift my chin, Malcolm says, "All you need to worry about is tonight. Right now. While I'm devouring your pussy, I'm gonna be fingering your tight asshole so I can take it before the sun comes up."

And my orgasm is back thanks to that threat. I've never had anal with anyone before, but the idea of being tied up while Malcolm licks me and stretches me is exciting. I can't wait to see what happens, because I know that anything Malcolm does to my body will feel good.

My fingers move faster on my clit, and he notices. "You like that idea?"

I moan around his cock and close my eyes as my pleasure builds and builds until my orgasm finally explodes like a rocket out of me.

"Fuck," I hear Malcolm say as I start to come back down and he finally withdraws his dick from my mouth. "I knew it. Your mouth has ruined me."

"I'm...not...apologizing," I tell him between gasps as I swipe my fingers over my lips to dry them.

"Of course not," he mutters. "And I'm not going to apologize for how I'm about to rip apart those yellow panties to get my mouth on your cunt."

"About time too. My jaw may never close right again," I joke, opening and closing it a few times.

"That mouth of yours is dangerous. Downright lethal. And I fucking love it," Malcolm says, not even flinching over his use of the l-word.

"You just love my lack of a gag reflex," I tell him as I start untying his boots to get them and his jeans all the way off.

"That too," he agrees while removing his cut and shirt over his head in one move, then tossing them to the floor. "It's impressive; but if I think about it too long, I may put a hole through the fucking wall."

"Naked and jealous is a good look on you, Malcolm," I tell him honestly as I let my eyes roam up his tattooed and muscular body.

My hands freeze on his second boot when he says, "I'm sure it would look good on you too if you ever met the women I've fucked before."

"Ugh, let's not talk about that."

Malcolm reaches down and pulls me to my feet. "I wish it had been me," he says, his big hand grasping my jaw as his eyes hold mine. "I wish it had been me that first day in the bar."

"Me too," I tell him honestly.

For a few silent seconds, I think he's going to say something else, something else sweet, like maybe declare his love for me. But instead, he hefts me up and over his shoulder without another word, and then neither of us are able to speak the English language for the rest of the night as Malcolm makes good on his threat.

CHAPTER NINETEEN

Malcolm

I get an earful from my boys the next day. Bobby G. and his crew split as soon as the boat docked last night; and needless to say, the merger was dead on arrival. I'm starting to think the guys may be right. When it comes to Naomi, I lose my cool and can't think straight. If I keep fucking things up because of her, I won't last as president. And the MC? Well, it's the only fucking family I've ever had. Nothing is more important to me. I refuse to sit around and watch it crumble from the inside out like the Ace of Spades MC did.

I need to make better decisions. Rational decisions that don't have anything to do with who I'm sleeping with every night.

Besides, my time with Naomi is almost over. We only have one more night together before our deal comes to an end. Then we're done and over. She'll go her way with the debt to Harry paid, and I'll stop thinking with my dick and start using my head to run shit again.

It sucks because I'm not ready to give her up yet. And the worst part is that I'm not sure if I would ever get enough of her even if I had years with her.

She's the best woman I've ever had in and out of bed.

While it won't be easy to forget her, I have no choice but to get the hell over her.

∼

Naomi

SOMETHING HAPPENED EARLIER today in the Aces' most recent meeting. I don't think it was anything good based on the way Malcolm's been watching me during my shift and putting away so much Jack Daniels that Ronnie seems worried we might run out.

"Everything okay?" I ask when I walk up to him at the bar and stand between his spread legs.

"Today's the end of your two weeks," Malcolm says coolly, keeping one hand on his bottle of Jack and the other on top of his thigh.

"Yeah, it is," I reply. I never would've thought that I could have so much fun with the outlaw biker. Now I'm glad I got caught stealing from him. "Should we celebrate hard tonight?"

"Tonight you need to come by the house and get your things," he says, throwing back the rest of his whiskey in one gulp.

"What do you mean?" I ask.

"The two weeks are up, so you need to move on, find work someplace else."

Putting my hand on my cocked hip, I say, "You want me to move on?"

"Yeah."

"Are you saying you want me to move on from you too?"

"That's right, honey. Move the fuck on," he slurs, the effects of the alcohol showing. "We're done. Time for you to get the hell off this gravy train."

Wow. I can't believe he just said that.

"So, the last two weeks were just satisfying a deal to you? Just fucking, nothing more?" I ask as tears blur my vision. His silence speaks volumes. "Wow, Malcolm. Guess I was wrong about you after all."

"Guess you were," he mutters, making me even angrier since he looks like he could care less that we're done and over.

"If we're done, does that mean I'm free to go back to fucking Fiasco?" I ask, trying to get some sort of response out of him.

One minute the empty bottle of Jack is there, and the next it's busting against the far wall as Malcolm jumps to his feet. "You stay the hell away from him!"

"Why do you care?" I ask. "Our two weeks are up and you're done with me."

"I'm serious, Naomi," he warns me.

"Maybe you two should fight again and see if he can win a turn to use me as his blowup doll for two weeks or two months."

"Don't fucking test me, woman."

"Or I could go sleep with the other four members of your MC, give them all a test drive to see who the best fuck is..."

He grabs my necklace to pull my face to his so swiftly that it snaps the clasp and he's left holding the charm and chain. "You are going to stay the hell away from all of us, do you hear me?"

"Fuck you, Malcolm," I seethe. "What Harry said about you was true. You are a cold, heartless bastard who deserved to be robbed."

Without another word, I storm off to the bathroom in the employee lounge to hide, bawling my eyes out as I sit on the closed toilet lid crying until we dock.

CHAPTER TWENTY

Malcolm

The next few weeks are fucking miserable. Naomi did what I told her to do — packed her shit and left without sparing me a backwards glance. My boys keep reminding me of how she was stealing from us and reassuring me that she was only after me for some easy money. They're trying to make me feel like a sucker and an easy mark, just another guy who fell for her pretty little bullshit. As the weeks pass, though, and my head clears from the drunken haze of the first lonely nights I've known in a long while, I start to have my doubts.

Naomi never asked me for anything.

I'm the one who made her the offer, and I'm the one who settled her debt with Harry. All of that was on me, my idea and my decision.

And her necklace with the outrageously expensive black diamonds? Well, after I broke her necklace the last night on the boat, she didn't even try to take it with her.

I keep trying to play back every interaction I had with Naomi in my head, and I'm convinced she never asked me for a dime. Yeah, she signed on with us with the intention of stealing, but she didn't know me from Jesus H. Christ at the time. Once she did, she never tried to run any scam on me.

I've gotten so used to the kinds of chicks that hang around the MC, looking to trap a brother with their pussies for an easy paycheck, that I've become cynical. Yeah, Naomi was in a fucked-up situation when we first met; but the more I think about it, the more I'm convinced there was more to her. More to us.

Now, if I only knew how to express that to her, or how to even begin sorting out the way I feel in her absence.

∽

Naomi

Fuck Malcolm Hyde. Fuck his temper-tantrums, fuck his club, fuck his bike, fuck his little house, fuck his beautiful hair, fuck the way he made me feel when I wrapped my arms around his waist and rode on the back of his motorcycle, fuck the way he made me feel when he wrapped his arms around my waist and rode me so goddamned well…

"Shit!" I cry out as I sit on my couch in my empty house. It's not working. I keep trying to get angry at him, to hate him for sending me away, but all I keep coming back to are good memories. Great memories, actually, of the time we spent together and what I was sure was something … something … god, I don't know. A relationship? After the way we started things off together? That would be impossible.

He could never trust me after the things I had done. Thinking about him all the time, even dreaming about him as I sleep, won't change things.

The next morning, almost three weeks after I walked out of Malcolm's house, I finally decide while I'm brushing my teeth that I'm going to forget about my beautiful, bad-ass biker crush and get on with my fucking life. No matter how bad it makes me feel, no matter how much it twists my guts up or how nauseous the thought makes me, I have to let him go.

Just as I've convinced myself that my stomach is revolting against me trying to move on with my life, I vomit explosively all over my sink!

"What the fuck?" I mutter as I hold my toothbrush away from me, spitting and teary-eyed from my sudden eruption. "I didn't even drink anything last night... Oh god, no," I mutter, desperately trying to think back over the last few weeks. I haven't been keeping up with my periods all that well, but I'm certain that my last one was...was before I ever got on Malcolm fucking Hyde's wild and wonderful ride.

"Oh for the love of God!" I cry as I shake my toothbrush at the ceiling. "Fuck you, fuck you, fuck you, Malcolm!"

Malcolm

I'VE BEEN RACKING my brain trying to figure out how to approach Naomi again and have damn near given myself an aneurysm trying to find the words to express how I'm feeling. How she has made me feel. I'm still so twisted up by the whole thing that other than working with Aces on the boat at night, I've been avoiding the club this past week.

Which is why I'm caught completely off guard when I come roaring up to my little beach shack on my bike one evening to find a collection of motorcycles I recognize as my crew's, along with what looks like some sort of delivery van sitting in my driveway. I'm not in the mood for company, but I at least owe my boys time to bend my ear before I throw them out of my house.

"HAPPY BIRTHDAY!" comes the cheering chorus when I storm into my small foyer, glaring around my living room at the other members of my MC and what can only be a half dozen women in varying degrees of undress. I don't know if they're professional strippers or just amateurs having a good time, but at least one of them is dancing on Fiasco in my favorite chair like she knows her way around a pole.

"Fuck, thanks guys," I sigh as I walk on into my house. "I've been so far up my own ass the last week I forgot this shit was coming up."

"Well, we didn't forget!" Devlin proclaims as he slaps Fiasco on the shoulder. "We would never let an opportunity for a party like this pass us by! Get your ass in here and meet your lovely guests!"

"Or maybe have a drink first," Nash offers as he holds out a brand-new bottle of Jack Daniels to me, complete with a little, red ribbon. "Take the edge off and relax, man. Things have a way of working out, if you don't force them too hard."

"Truer words," I mumble in an informal toast as I crack open the bottle and take a long pull. "Fuck it," I mutter when I come up for air. "You're all here now, so take me around and do the introductions. You girls came all the way out here to see me, so you might as well have a good time!"

*

Naomi

SINCE I CAN'T SLEEP ANYWAY, I wait up for when Malcolm would usually get home, and then I gather up my courage, driving over to his house. I have no idea what I'm going to say or how to explain things when I see him again, but I know we have to talk.

When I pull up to his house, I can see his motorcycle is there, along with several others and what looks like a catering van. I really didn't want to talk to him with any sort of an audience, but I can't make myself leave without at least seeing him first.

When I walk up the stairs to his screen door, I can hear the music rattling the windows, and it takes several minutes of knocking before he finally throws open the door.

When Malcolm finally answers, he just stands there in shock, looking as though he's completely lost for words. Finally, he asks, "What are you doing here, Naomi?"

"We need to talk," I say as I slip inside his small beach house and find several other members of the MC lounging around the living room with mostly naked women draped all over them.

Wow. I mean, I didn't think he had been celibate for the last few weeks, but knowing Malcolm is sleeping with other women and then seeing it in person is a slap in the face I wasn't ready for.

"Well?" Malcolm says as he steps in front of where I'm standing completely frozen in place, staring at all of his visitors. "Talk or get naked." He crowds me until my back hits the foyer wall, and then his hand is on my thigh, snaking its way up underneath my loose summer dress. "I'll give you three guesses to pick the one I would prefer."

His words are slurred, and I can smell the stench of alcohol on his breath. Maybe I should leave and come back to do this another time.

No, no, I have to tell him now. I have to tell someone, and he's all I've got. I grab his wrist to stop his hand's progress before he reaches my panties. Not because I don't want him touching me there, but because I can't sleep with him without telling him why I'm here.

"We *have* to talk," I reiterate.

"Anything you need to say to me, you can say in front of my boys," Malcolm replies.

Without letting his wrist go, I drag him back outside to his porch. He staggers but follows me willingly, leaving the front door open. This isn't the kind of conversation I want others to overhear, so I close it for him.

Before I can figure out what I'm going to say, how to go about telling him this, Malcolm reaches forward and runs his index fingertip along the V-neck of my dress, dipping it into the cleavage. "I've missed these titties."

Of course he missed my body and being able to use it whenever he wanted. Not that I have anything to complain about since I enjoyed being with him too. But he hasn't said he missed me, the rest of the parts he can't fuck.

When Malcolm leans forward and runs his warm, wet tongue down into my cleavage, I involuntarily moan as my body lights up all over. Damn him for being so good at distracting me by hijacking my body. The fact that he has hijacked my body in more than one way is what has me putting on the brakes.

"Malcolm," I say, grabbing both sides of his bearded face to pull up and try to make him stop. But he just cups both of my swollen, sensitive tits in his hands and keeps tonguing my boobs more enthusiastically. "Malcolm, please stop."

"In a minute," is what he slurs before his mouth goes back to work, turning up the heat on my hormones so quickly that I get dizzy and stumble a step backward, nearly falling down the steps.

"Malcolm, I'm pregnant!" I exclaim as I tug roughly on his hair to pull his mouth away from my boobs.

That declaration definitely stops him in his tracks.

"You...what?" he asks, his hazy, green eyes meeting mine. God, I really hope he remembers this conversation in the morning, because I don't know if I can do it again.

"I'm pregnant."

He stares down at me silently for several seconds, and then laughs. "Get the fuck outta here!" With a wave of his hand, he dismisses my confession, either because he thinks I'm joking or doesn't give a shit. Only after he pulls out a cigarette, lights it up and takes a drag does he add, "Are you fucking with me, Naomi?"

"No, Malcolm. I'm not fucking with you. I'm pregnant, and it's yours."

"No. No fucking way," he mutters as he sucks on his cancer stick and shakes his head in denial.

"I am. I got sick and I was late, so I took a bunch of tests, and all of them were positive."

"So, what you're saying is that you lied to me," he replies, his face going from slack and horny drunk to narrowed eyed and angry in the blink of my watery eyes.

"What are you talking about?" I ask. "I didn't lie to you."

"Yeah, you did," he says, blowing smoke out of his nose like an enraged bull. "You told me you were on the pill, and you weren't."

"Yes, I was on the pill," I assure him. "You saw them! I just...I missed one the night you brought me home and then was late the next night because of the fight when I was too pissed at you to remember to go home and get them!"

"Right. You just *forgot* to take them," Malcolm clips out sarcastically. "And even after you 'forgot' to take them, you still told me to fucking come inside of you!"

"I had never missed any pills before...I didn't think it was a big deal as long as I eventually took them!"

"You didn't know that, if I filled your pussy with cum, you would get knocked up, and then I would be on the hook for fucking child support for the next eighteen goddamn years?" he yells at me.

"I didn't do this on purpose, Malcolm," I tell him as tears roll down both of my cheeks.

"Oh, bullshit!"

"I didn't!" I scream at the top of my lungs. "And I don't want your money! That's not why I'm here telling you! I'm telling you, because...because you're going to be his or her father, you drunk asshole!"

Turning away from me, Malcolm goes over to the railing. He

leans over it on his elbows with his head bowed, his long hair hiding his face. Puffs of smoke occasionally float through the air before he straightens up and puts the cigarette out on the rail.

When he finally faces me again, his jaw clenched tight, he removes his wallet from his back pocket and pulls out a wad of hundred-dollar bills, offering them to me. "Here's enough for an abortion."

"What?" I gasp, outraged that he would blurt that out without asking or caring what I want, not to mention try and throw cash at me for it.

"If it's not about the money, then prove it – end it. Get rid of it."

"Screw you, Malcolm! I'm not doing that," I tell him with an adamant shake of my head. It only took me about ten seconds of consideration after the stick turned blue for me to reach that verdict. Still, I *did* consider it. God knows it would make everything so much easier, but I don't know if I could live with that guilt.

"That's what I fucking thought," he says as he runs his fingers through his hair to push it out of his face.

"I just...I wish it was that easy, I do. But I can't do that," I try to explain to him. "I'm going to have this baby, and I'll do it on my own if I need to. I just thought that you would want to know..."

"I already knew you were a goddamn gold-digger. This shit only validates that!"

Swiping away the dampness from under each of my eyes, I tell him, "I really hope this is the alcohol talking and not you."

"Surprisingly, as soon as you said you were pregnant, I sobered right the hell up," he mutters. "Not exactly the happy fucking birthday I was hoping for."

Today's his birthday? I had no idea. Would I have still come if I had known? No, I would've waited. But it's too late; and since there's nothing left to say and I refuse to stand on his porch listening to him call me names, I jog down the front steps to my car without another word, without accepting his stupid money.

"I'm getting a fucking DNA test before I pay a fucking penny!" Malcolm yells at my back.

I want to flip him off or yell at him and blame him for putting me in this position.

But he's right. It's my own damn fault for being late taking a few days' worth of my pills.

And now I wish I had never slept with Malcolm fucking Hyde.

∼

Malcolm

"WHAT THE HELL WAS THAT ABOUT?" Nash asks when I walk back inside my house like a zombie after the bomb Naomi just dropped on me. "We could hear you yelling over the music. Sounded like all hell broke loose."

"Yeah, it did," I tell him. Grabbing the bottle of beer from his hand, I throw it back and then wipe my mouth on the back of my hand before handing it back. "She's knocked up and says it's mine."

"Oh, fuck that noise!" he huffs. "You getting a test?"

"Yeah, that's what I told her, but it probably is mine."

"Are you serious? You fucked her bareback?" Nash asks. "How stupid could you be? You knew she was a lying thief you couldn't trust!"

"Yeah, I know," I agree. "I'm an idiot for choosing a few seconds of pleasure over common fucking sense."

"A few seconds?" he teases.

"Shut the fuck up. You know what I mean."

Slapping his hand on my shoulder, he says, "Yeah, I do. But maybe you're wrong and it's someone else's..."

I don't even consider that option for a second because it makes me too fucking furious picturing Naomi with someone else.

As if on cue, Fiasco chooses that moment to walk up to us. "What's going on, Prez?" he asks.

"Naomi's pregnant," I inform him.

"Oh shit," Fiasco mutters, his face going pale. Then even louder, he says, "Oh shit! Is it...could it be mine?"

"No, you dumbass. You can't impregnate a woman by coming in her mouth!" I snap at him, mostly angry at Naomi and myself, not him. But he's here right now, and it's nice to have someone else to take it out on.

"Oh, right," the idiot replies with a slap of his palm to his forehead. "I'm so fucking wasted right now."

"What's your excuse every other day of the week?" Nash teases him, but I don't hear the rest of their conversation or anyone else's before the sun comes up.

All I can do is keep thinking about Naomi, how much I missed her before she showed up and told me she was having my kid. Now, I'll never know if she gave a shit about me or if she only slept with me to screw me over.

CHAPTER TWENTY-ONE

Naomi

Over the next few months, I blow up at record-breaking speed. The comfort eating probably isn't helping, but I tell myself I should stuff my face with whatever my body is craving for the growing baby inside of me.

Malcolm's baby.

Not that he'll ever probably see him or her since he wants no part of me or it. He made that perfectly clear when he tried to throw a few hundred dollars at me so that I would get rid of it.

I dip my last crispy crinkle fry into ketchup during my early lunch break and then call back to the kitchen, "Another order of fries, Jacob!" before I've even finished chewing.

"Coming right up," our cook says through the serving window.

"Is it going to be another one of those days?" Nancy asks.

"Another what kind of day?"

"You know, where you cry all day and customers think you've lost your pregnant mind."

"No," I huff, even though I can't make any guarantees. "I'm just hungry this morning."

"It's five minutes after ten o'clock in the morning, and you're on your second serving of fries."

"So?" I ask defensively. "I'm going to have a veggie plate for dinner with fruits for dessert."

"Strawberry ice cream doesn't count as a fruit."

"The kid needs dairy too!" I exclaim.

"Sure, it does. Apparently, every drop from a dairy farm, but whatever floats your boat," she says with a grin.

The word boat automatically has me thinking about Malcolm, wondering how he's been doing, who he's been screwing over the desk in his office since I'm no longer available. Probably Anika or Ronnie. Maybe both at the same time. He was good at multi-tasking.

And while he's having fun doing whoever and whatever he wants, I'm gaining weight at the rate of what feels like a pound a day and am completely un-fuckable since I'm the size of a cow. My udders are even sagging when before they were so small and perky, I didn't need to even wear a bra.

My new, rotund figure aside, there are a million other worries that are much more important at the moment. For instance, I could barely make ends meet before I got knocked up. Now, I'm trying to scrape by to afford the basics for the baby like somewhere for it to sleep, a few clothes for it to wear, blankets and bottles. The list of necessities seems endless.

There's also the baby's health that keeps me up at night. It seems so small and fragile, like everything and anything could hurt it. Since I've been going for free checkups at the health department, I've only had one ultrasound to make sure there was a heartbeat, which there was, thumping loud and clear over the speakers. I won't get to see my baby on a scan for another few weeks, and it sucks.

The days go by so slowly, but too quickly at the same time.

And while I'm not a medical doctor, I think this constant miserable emotion hanging over my head like a grey cloud is severe depression.

~

Malcolm

I'VE KEPT myself busy for the past few months, refusing to give in to the desire to check in on Naomi. Mostly, I was afraid that I'm so weak for her that just seeing her face would have me asking her to come back into my life.

Which would be stupid.

I'm better off without her.

At least that's what I keep telling myself constantly, and it's what I'm thinking about one day when I stop at a local gas station in the middle of town to fill up my bike.

While I'm waiting for the pump to cut off, I glance around at the strip mall across the street, and that's when I spot her.

The first thing I notice is her belly, answering one of the burning questions on my mind. Fuck. She's still determined to have this kid. I want to hate her for not taking the easy way out, for still planning to drag me through the hell of lawyers and courtrooms as she comes after me for child support. But mostly I'm pissed because I didn't know what she had decided, and I missed out on so many months with her that I barely recognize her now.

Then, I realize that she's not just popping into the twenty-four-hour restaurant to eat but to work. She's wearing a uniform, carrying trays of food when she should be at home with her feet up, resting as she grows a human.

Walking inside the gas station, I pour myself a cup of coffee because I'm not ready to leave yet and I'm trying to talk myself out of walking across the street. Then, I just stand at the second window watching her run around on her feet for what feels like an eternity. She stops only occasionally for something to drink and eat while clutching her belly the whole time like it hurts.

Is she okay?

Is the baby okay?

"Dude," a guy says when he walks up behind where I'm standing with my arms crossed over my chest, still staring out the same window again a few days later. "I let the first hour slide, but now this stalking thing you're doing has gone on long enough. Am I really gonna have to call the cops to make you leave?"

I glare over my shoulder to see who the hell is speaking to me. It's the skinny kid who runs the gas station register, and my enraged face dares him to call the police. "What the fuck do you care if I stand here? I'm not in anyone's way, and I buy gas and a carton of smokes every day when I come in," I point out defensively.

"Who are you looking at?" he asks, strolling up right beside me so that our shoulders are almost touching, not the least bit intimidated by me. Guess he's grown a pair of balls after probably getting robbed at least a few times a year in this joint.

"None of your fucking business," I snap at him.

"The blonde?" he asks. "Her face is hot if you can get past the gut..."

"She's pregnant, dipshit!"

"Oh," he says. Putting his face closer to the glass and squinting, he says, "Yeah, I can see that now. My bad. Is it yours?"

I don't respond.

"Why are we watching your baby mama from here instead of just going into the restaurant?" he asks. "It's a public place too."

"*We* aren't doing shit," I remark. "And I don't want to see her."

"Three days man. Today is the third day in a row you've come to see her, so I think what you mean is that you don't *want* to talk to her."

"Nothing to say."

"You could start with, 'Hi, honey. Big baby stomach you've got there. I miss you. Do you miss me?'"

"Fuck off," I tell him, even though it's a little eerie how he nailed my nickname for her down like that.

"I would fuck off, man, really I would. But you see, this is actually *my* store. That's why I came up to you just now, to tell *you* to fuck off or I'm gonna call the cops and report you as a creeper."

"You really own this store?" I ask in surprise since he's younger than me.

"Yeah. My father gave it to me a year back when he retired. Wants to keep it in the family, you know?"

"No, I don't know."

"About the father part or family business part?"

"Neither."

"Wow, that's surprising," the kid says with a low whistle.

"What the hell are you talking about?" I grumble.

"Of all people, I would think you growing up without a dad, knowing firsthand about what the emptiness of not having a parent in your life feels like, would make you determined to be a part of your son or daughter's life."

"Fuck off," I tell him again because I don't need his judgment.

"Whatever," he says, walking over behind us to grab a pack of M&Ms from the closest shelve and come back. He rips it open and dumps a handful in his palm, then tosses them into his mouth. "Getting pissed at me doesn't solve any of your problems, dude. You've got bigger fish to fry. Like the fact that sometimes your baby mama only buys three dollars' worth of gas and pays for it in change."

"What the fuck?" I exclaim, not liking that he knows so much about her or that she's living on change.

"She's flat broke. Pretty sure she stuffs toilet paper from the bathroom under her shirt sometimes too. That's why I didn't know for sure she was pregnant."

"You're screwing with me, aren't you?"

"Nope. Can't make this shit up," he says. "It's depressing. I'd help Naomi out if I could; but if I gave a handout to every pretty face that comes through here, I would go out of business fast."

"Wait. How the hell do you know her name?" I ask him.

He makes me wait until he tosses more candy into his mouth and chews them up before answering. "Calm down, dude. She wears a nametag."

"Oh. Right." I clear my throat as I consider my next question for him. "Does she...have you ever seen her with any men?"

He cocks his head to the side, carefully considering that inquiry before finally giving me a response. "Nope. I don't think so. Some guys think the belly is hot, but most aren't about trying to get in the middle of all that parental responsibility, no matter how hot she is. Not to mention she always looks pretty miserable, like there's not enough caffeine in the world to perk her up."

"Sounds like you've thought about her quite a lot," I point out in a grumble.

"Eh, I have a lot of free time on my hands."

"Obviously."

"So, what's the plan, man? You gonna keep standing here every day watching her or what?"

"I don't know," I answer honestly.

"I'll give you the first...fifteen minutes free, but after that I'm gonna have to start charging you a stalker fee each day."

"A stalker fee?" I repeat in disbelief.

"Think of it like rent. If you're going to keep coming in here all grumpy, taking up space in my store, then I'm gonna need you to offset the loss of customers who see your sourpuss in the window and drive away to the gas station up the road. You know, the one that doesn't have grumpy men lurking around all the time."

"Fine. How much?" I ask.

"Twenty bucks an hour."

"That's robbery," I tell him. "Ten bucks an hour, and I'll spend at least twenty bucks while I'm here."

"Deal. But you owe me back sourpuss rent for yesterday and the day before. As well as today."

"Will you keep tabs on her for me when I'm not here?" I ask as I pull out my wallet and start counting out bills.

"It'll cost you extra."

"Whatever," I huff, knowing what I'm doing is downright insane but unsure how the hell to make myself stop.

CHAPTER TWENTY-TWO

Naomi

"Lovely night tonight, isn't it?" Greg, the gas station attendant, asks when I bring a gallon of milk and a Hershey bar up to the counter.

"Ah, yeah. Sure," I reply, glad someone is in a good mood.

"Anything else for you?"

"I, ah, I need five dollars in gas on pump number three."

"Why not fill her up tonight? It's on the house," he says with a grin.

"What?" I ask in confusion, tired after working twelve hours, my feet so swollen I can only shuffle them, not pick them up even an inch.

"You're a valued customer; and to show how much I appreciate your business, tonight's full tank of gas is on me."

"Seriously? That's like...twenty-five dollars' worth."

"It's fine. Really."

I stare at the kid and wait for him to tell me the catch.

Oh no.

Does he think I'm gonna screw him for a full tank of gas? Sure, I've had tough times, but I can't imagine ever being that desperate. Not to mention that I promised myself I will *never* exchange sex for anything, especially money, after how badly everything went to hell with Malcolm.

Lowering my voice, I tell him, "I'm-I'm sorry, but I'm not gonna sleep with you for gasoline."

"God no!" he exclaims. "I'm not trying to get myself murdered."

"Huh?"

"Nothing," he says in a rush. "The gas doesn't come with any strings attached. Promise."

"You're sure?" I ask.

"Yep."

"Well, um, that's okay then I guess," I reply.

Chuckling as he rings up my items, he says, "You're a funny girl, Naomi."

For a moment, I freeze when he says my name so familiarly. Then I remember I'm still in my uniform with my nametag, just like his.

"I appreciate your kindness, Greg." I slide a five-dollar bill across the counter for my milk and candy bar before snatching the goods up, ready to get the hell out of here and get home to my bed. "Keep the change and, ah, have a good night."

"You too!" he calls out as I hurry out of the store.

∽

There's something about my interaction with the gas station guy that I can't shake the rest of the night. In fact, I'm still replaying our conversation the next morning.

"Hey, Nancy," I say to my boss when my shift starts, and the breakfast crowd has thinned out. "Do you ever get gas from the place across the street?"

"Yeah, why?" she responds while tying her graying red hair up in a messy bun.

"Does Greg give you stuff for free?"

"Who's Greg?"

"The guy who works there."

"Oh. No. Why? Do you get shit for free?" she asks.

"Ah, well, yeah. Last night he gave me a full tank of gas when I bought milk and a candy bar."

She eyes my belly. "Must be trying to get in your pregnant panties."

"No, I don't think that's it at all," I tell her. "He doesn't even stare at my boobs."

"Huh," she mutters. "Only you would waste time worrying about why someone gave you something for free."

"Yeah. It's stupid," I agree with a shake of my head. "Anyway, I've been meaning to ask you something. Your daughter Beth is eighteen now, right?"

"Yeah. Why?" she asks with an arched red eyebrow.

"I was wondering, what are her plans when she graduates from school?"

"Nothing. Not a damn thing at the moment, no matter how many times I ask her," she huffs.

"Oh, well, do you think she may be interested in being my nanny after the baby's born?"

"Maybe. I could ask her. I'm guessing the pay would be shit?" she remarks with a grin.

"Less than shit," I admit with a blush. "But she could come live with me, free room and board and meals if there's food in the fridge and cabinets."

"I'd pay *you* to get her out of my house. I'm tired of arguing with her over every little thing like who ate the last muffin or why isn't her favorite pair of jeans washed when she just wore them yesterday!"

"That sounds...annoying. Still, I could put up with washing her clothes and buying her endless muffins if she could just keep an eye on the baby while I work at night."

"So all she would have to do is get up with the brat if it starts crying in the middle of the night and you'll be home during the day?"

"That's my plan," I agree. It's not a great one; but with limited options, it's the best I can come up with.

"I'll talk to her and let you know."

"Thanks, Nancy," I tell her.

"Yeah, yeah. Who can say no to the sad woman who is eighty months pregnant?"

"I'm only five months along!"

Eying my baby bump, she says, "Could've fooled me."

CHAPTER TWENTY-THREE

Malcolm

"What's new?" I ask Greg when I waltz into the gas station one Friday afternoon before reporting to the boat.

"Apparently not your approach," he replies with a grin. "It's been, what, three months and you still haven't gone to talk to her face to face?"

"I don't need to talk to her," I huff as I take up my usual position in front of the window. Lately, I just drop by for a few minutes, not letting myself stay too long because it's not good for my mental health. Trying to abstain turned out to be even worse. "I'm just checking in to make sure she's okay."

"Does she look okay to you?" he asks as he leaves his post behind the counter to come stand beside me.

"I don't know..."

"Because to me she looks like that blueberry chick from Willy Wonka. Well, except she's all red-faced and sweaty."

"Give her a break! She's, like, eight months pregnant by now!" I remind him.

Grabbing a pack of Twizzler's from the shelf, Greg rips the wrapper open and goes at the red candy. "You feel guilty for doing that to her. I don't blame you. That's a tough row to hoe."

"What the fuck did you just say?"

Taking another bite of his Twizzler, he goes on to tell me, "You're right to blame yourself. I would too. I mean, for you, it was what, just one hot night of pleasure? And for her, well, nine months is a long time to have your body taken over by a parasitic alien."

"It was more than one time," I remark. "Usually more than once in a night."

"Bareback more than once, huh? So you don't even know which time it was that did the trick, sealing her fate as a single mother and yours as a lonely, creepy stalker."

"I don't even know for sure it's mine," I tell him.

"Yeah, right. Could be any number of the men who come and watch her from afar like pathetic losers for months on end."

"I'm gonna fucking kill you for running your mouth one of these days," I warn him, but he just keeps chewing, completely unfazed. I know a lot of stone-cold killers, but all of them would envy this odd convenience store clerk's composure. Not for the first time, I wonder what kind of shit this dude has seen that completely deadened his nerves. With a huff, I ask him, "Why do you think she hasn't asked me for a DNA test yet?"

"I don't know," he replies. "Maybe because she doesn't want you in the baby's life."

When a low growl escapes me at hearing that infuriating notion, he holds up his palms, waving his Twizzler at me and says, "You asked the question, dude. Not my fault if you don't like my answer."

"If she wants my money, then she has to let me in their life."

"Maybe she doesn't want your money either," he says. "Again, that's just a possibility, not a judgment."

"What woman wouldn't want my money?" I ask.

"One who doesn't think that putting up with you is worth it."

"She obviously needs help!" I exclaim. "She works twelve hours a damn day in a diner and lives in a rundown hellhole!"

"Tell that to her, not me. If it were me, I would definitely carry your kid for eighteen years of cash."

"Fuck off," I tell him.

"Look, dude, she's not going to be like this for much longer. Soon, she'll pop the kid out, and her body will get hot as hell again, and then men will want her even with the screaming baby around. If you ask me, now is about the best chance you'll have to get her back, before she has options again."

"Do you know how many women I could have right now if I wanted them?" I tell him.

"Dozens? Hundreds? How would I know? I've got bad teeth and I run a gas station. I don't have a lot of experience getting attention from women. I have to actually work for it."

"A lot. As many as I wanted."

"But none of them are her, right? Which is why you would rather watch her from across the street than take one of the others to bed. Sort of pathetic for you, but I've never been in love. Maybe this is just how it makes people act."

"I don't love her," I argue with a scoff. "We were only screwing around together for a few weeks."

"How long does it take to fall in love? Some people say it happens in seconds when it's love at first sight. Why not a few weeks?"

"You sound like the biggest pussy on the planet," I tell him.

"Says the man who has been pining away for his baby mama for months and hasn't done a damn thing about it. Do your bros know how pussy whipped you are for pussy you're not even getting inside?"

"Fuck you, Greg."

"Hey, I got laid last night," he says. "Be honest with me, when was the last time you bumped uglies with a woman?"

"You're full of shit, and that's none of your goddamn business."

"So, in other words, Naomi was the last woman you banged eight or so months ago. How sad is your dick right now?"

"Shut up," I tell him with a sigh. As if I actually expect my words to stop his mouth from running. Just like Naomi, Greg isn't scared of me, and nothing I do seems to intimidate him.

"That bastard is probably ready to mutiny," he continues. "Does it even work anymore, or did she take your balls away from you too?"

"Low blow, Greg. Low fucking blow."

But he's right. Naomi owns every part of me and has for months now, even though I've tried to move on. It's impossible. I can't forget her, especially since I know she's carrying my kid. Yet, for some reason, whether it's pride or fear, I can't figure out how to go about getting her back.

I thought she was a distraction I didn't need, and then I was certain she intentionally got knocked up because she's a thief who prefers to take money rather than earn it.

Now I just feel like a giant asshole who is so twisted that I don't know which way is up. My closest friend the past few weeks has been Gas Station Greg. He's the only person I can talk to; I can't even begin to explain to my boys what I'm going through.

And yeah, maybe I'm pissed at the guys because they are all free to screw whoever they want; but as soon as I sleep with a woman and feel protective of her, they think I'm going to run the entire MC into the ground. It's not fair that I'm held to a higher standard just because I'm the president.

While the MC has always been the most important thing in the world, and that probably won't change anytime soon, I can't help but feel like maybe there's room for something else in my life too.

If only I could figure out how to get it back.

CHAPTER TWENTY-FOUR

Naomi

This morning it took me twice as long to get ready because of the pain in my lower back. In fact, it's so bad that I haven't even been at work for ten minutes before I escape to the bathroom to sit down on the toilet seat in one of the stalls while I wait for the cramping to stop.

Last night, when I got home from work, I couldn't sleep, so I put together the crib I got from a consignment shop. Guess I must have pulled a muscle in the process.

The ache does stop, temporarily, before it comes right back just as strong or maybe even worse than before.

And finally, after half an hour of the on-again, off-again pain does the realization of what's going on finally hit me.

I think I'm in labor.

Pulling a wad of toilet paper from the roll, I sob like a baby into it because I'm not ready for this! My due date is still two weeks away. I thought I would have more time to prepare for the baby, emotionally and physically. Other than the crib and a few outfits, I haven't even bought bottles or diapers!

I'm already a horrible mother, and my daughter hasn't even come into the world yet.

The bathroom door opens, so I try to quiet down my bawling.

"Naomi?" Nancy asks. "Are you okay?"

"Y-yeah?" I respond, but it comes out sounding like more of a question than a statement.

"You don't sound okay, and you've been in here for almost an hour!" she calls back. "Don't you dare have that baby in one of our toilets!"

"I won't. I'm not," I promise her.

The restroom door slowly swings in since I didn't lock it, and then Nancy, the one person I can always count on to be a ballbuster, offering no pity to anyone, looks at me with a frown. Our eyes meet right as another pain hits. This one is so brutal I have to reach out and squeeze the roll of toilet paper, my nails digging into the tissue until the worst passes.

"You're having contractions, aren't you?" Nancy asks.

"No. Yes. I'm not sure," I lie, peeling off some tissue to blot at my tear and snot-soaked face once the worst passes.

"Come on, girl. Let's get you to the hospital."

"No! I can't!" I tell her with a shake of my head. "I'm not ready to do this. Maybe-maybe it's false-labor, you know, like Braxton Hicks contractions or something."

"Does it feel like your body is about to be ripped in half from your spine?"

"Sort of," I nod my agreement.

"Then you're in labor. That baby is coming any second now, so it would be great if you didn't make a mess for me to clean up in the bathroom."

"I'm sorry," I tell her as I start sobbing again.

"Don't apologize. Just get your ass up and in my car!"

"I can't!"

"Well, what the hell are you waiting for?" she asks, crossing her arms over her chest and sighing heavily when another teeth-clenching contraction hits me. That's right. I'm finally able to admit to myself that perhaps I am having contractions.

Once I'm able to breathe easily again without the agony, I clutch my belly and tell Nancy, "I'm not sure if I can do this."

"Not much of a choice now, girl. The baby's coming, and being in denial isn't going to stop it."

"I'm not ready!" I yell at her, like it's her fault that an asshole biker knocked me up and then tossed me aside like rotten leftovers he had found lurking in the fridge. "I can't...I don't know how to be a mother!"

"None of us do until the doctor puts the baby in our arms and says congratulations," Nancy tells me. "A more appropriate saying from the doc would be *good fucking luck*, because being a mother is *not* easy. Most of the time it's pretty damn hard, but the fact is anyone can do it. All it takes is one little skill."

"What's that?" I hiccup.

"Do you love her?" she asks.

"Yes."

"You already love this child who kicks you all night and has been leeching off of your body, your energy, your soul for almost nine months?"

"Yes," I answer again. I already care about this tiny person I've never met, more than myself. Loving her has never even been a question. If anything, I feel like I've let her down, not being the mother she deserves, one who could figure out how to keep her father around so that she wouldn't be raised like I was.

At least I was lucky enough to have my grandparents. This little girl only has me. No matter what it takes, I'll find a way to love her enough for the family she's missing.

"Then that's it!" Nancy says. "Loving her is all it takes for you to be a good mother. All you can do is keep loving your kid no matter what happens, and you'll figure it out. That's all this baby really needs from you."

"Okay," I say, trusting that she's right about this. "I think…I think I'm ready to go to the hospital."

"Finally! I thought I was going to have to knock you out and drag you in," she huffs with a roll of her eyes.

CHAPTER TWENTY-FIVE

Malcolm

Greg's ringing up a customer when I waltz into the store, so I grab a pack of chewing gum from the shelf, tear the package open and pop a piece into my mouth before I take up my usual position in front of the second window.

By the time Greg finishes the transaction and joins me, I still haven't spotted Naomi. Her car's in the parking lot, so she must be in the kitchen or in the bathroom.

"How's it going?" Greg asks.

A grunt is my response as I keep my eyes on the diner.

"She's not there," he tells me.

"What are you talking about?" I turn to ask him. "Her piece of shit car is right there," I tell him, pointing my finger at the old Chevy.

"She left. That other waitress, Nancy, peeled out of there with her about two hours ago. They were in a hell of a hurry to get somewhere."

"Are you fucking kidding me?" I exclaim in his face. "Why didn't you call and tell me?"

"Dude, I don't have your phone number! And it's not like you go more than a day without stopping in to check on her."

"Fuck," I say, dropping the pack of gum on the floor as I jog to the door.

"Think she's having the baby?" Greg calls out. I flip him off on the way outside to my bike.

Why didn't I give the kid my phone number so he could call me if something happened? I guess I thought Naomi had more time before she popped the kid out, but maybe not.

I ride by the farmhouse and knock on the door just to make sure Nancy didn't drop her off at home, but the place is empty.

There's only one other place Naomi could've gone.

I roar down the gravel driveway, taking off toward the hospital, breaking every moving violation known to man to get there within five minutes. Since it's a small town, the entire medical center, emergency room and all, is only about a hundred rooms on two floors. The second is where the labor and delivery is located; so once I'm on the elevator, I push the button frantically to get up there.

As soon as the elevator doors open, I can hear her screams. Halfway down the hallway I finally hear her voice after months.

"Please!" she begs. "Give me something, *anything* to make it stop!"

I'm standing just outside the door when a man's voice tells her, "I'm sorry, Naomi, but it's too late for an epidural. The baby's coming. Just a few more pushes and you'll get to see your little girl."

A girl.

I'm about to have a daughter.

The thought blows my mind. The faceless kid in my head now has Naomi's blonde hair and blue eyes, and she's wearing a bunch of pink shit. She's beautiful like her mother...

I hold on to that image in my mind for the next half an hour as I stand there listening to nothing but Naomi's pleas and screams that have me ready to strangle the doctor's throat. He said a few more pushes, which was obviously bullshit!

The only reason I don't kill him is because I sure as fuck don't know anything about birthing a baby, and I'm not sure if anyone else in this whole hospital does either, not the nurse in the room or the other woman who looks vaguely familiar. She's an older lady I finally realize I've seen lots of times in the diner. For all I know, this doc could be the only one in the entire city who can do this.

"Keep breathing. You're doing great," he tells Naomi calmly, like her face isn't a shade of red bordering on purple and there's not a gallon of sweat dripping down her forehead.

"Time to push," the nurse says. "Come on, you can do better than that. Push!"

"If I ever see...Malcolm Hyde again... I'm going to... *KILL HIM!*" Naomi yells before her words turn into an agonized scream.

She's right. I did this even though I put all the blame on her. What woman would willingly do this to her body, though? I don't think there's any amount of money in the world worth this kind of pain.

Suddenly, there's silence in the room, followed by the small cries of a baby.

"You did it!" the doctor says. "Congratulations! Here's your perfect and healthy baby girl."

Knowing it's over, that the pain is over for Naomi and that our daughter is healthy has my back sagging against the closest wall and saying a prayer to a god I'm not even sure I believe in.

I remain in the same spot, unmoving until the doctor walks out of the room, giving me a double-take with the nurse right behind him.

The next time I sneak a peek into the room, the baby's wrapped in a blanket in Naomi's arms. Tears are running down her cheeks, but she's also...smiling.

How the hell can she be happy about this when she was just screaming in pain?

"So, what do you think? Was she worth the nine months of

discomfort and hours of spine-snapping pain?" the other woman asks Naomi as she leans over to brush her knuckle over the baby's cheek.

"She's...amazing," Naomi responds with a sniffle. "I can't believe she's finally here."

"Still love her?"

"So much my heart feels like it may explode," she replies, making me feel like the biggest idiot in the world.

∼

Naomi

I HAVE A DAUGHTER.

I'm a mother.

While just hours ago those two things seemed like the scariest ideas in the world, now I know I can do this. I knew it as soon as I stared down at the pair of blue eyes that are gazing up at me in wonder.

"I'll give you two a little time together before they come get her for her bath," Nancy says.

"Thank you," I tell her, barely looking away from my little girl for more than a second. "For everything."

"No problem," she says as she walks out.

"Well, it's just you and me, baby girl," I tell her aloud. It doesn't even feel strange talking to her like she can understand me. She hears me, and soon she'll recognize my voice as her mother, if she can't already. "But don't worry. We've got this. I promise you we do, no matter what."

Before, I worried that a baby would be an extra expense and stress I didn't need. But holding her, she makes all my worries disappear because she's mine and I'm hers. It's us against the world; and while I wish she could grow up with a father, I'll keep telling myself we're better off without him.

And maybe one day I'll actually believe that statement is true.

CHAPTER TWENTY-SIX

Malcolm

As soon as Naomi and the baby go home from the hospital, I keep an eye on the farmhouse, stopping once in the morning in my truck and then at night after the boat docks when I stop by on my bike. Most of the time I don't even get a glimpse of them, but sometimes I do. For a few seconds, when I see her in the window, it's worth the hassle.

I keep waiting for a letter to come from an attorney, demanding a DNA sample to prove I'm the baby's father so Naomi can start collecting child support.

But I still haven't heard a single word.

And it blows my mind when I spot Naomi's car at the diner less than two weeks after she gave birth – and then Greg confirms that she's been there for hours, working a goddamn shift.

"Is she insane or something?" I ask him as we stand shoulder to shoulder at the window staring across the street. "Why would she leave the baby already? She's still tiny and needs her mama."

"If I had to guess," Greg starts, pausing to throw some M&Ms in his mouth. "The fact is that the bills don't give a shit about how little your kid is. They still have to be paid."

"I don't like it," I tell him.

"Then do something about it!"

"Like what, exactly?"

"Don't ask me, dude. I'm not the one who goes around knocking up poor women and then kicking them to the curb."

"That's not what I did," I say even though it sort of is. "We had a two-week deal. That's all it was supposed to be. This wasn't supposed to happen..."

"Plans change, shit happens. You've got to suck it up and roll with it, dude."

"Wait," I say as a thought hits me. "If Naomi's here, then who's watching the kid?"

"Like I would know?" Greg chuckles.

"Right. See ya," I tell him as I head out on my bike, riding to the farmhouse where there are no cars parked in the driveway. I kill the engine on my bike and stroll up to the rundown front porch as I begin to worry that Naomi left the baby home alone.

She wouldn't do that, would she?

Before I can peek into the living room, the front door opens and out strolls a young redheaded girl with earbuds in her ears and a full trash bag in her hand. I freeze, hoping she won't see me lurking behind the waist-high bushes beside the porch. And while it does take her a few seconds to notice me, eventually she startles, nearly jumping back a foot on the sidewalk as she shrieks and pulls her earbuds out.

"Who the hell are you?" she asks.

"Nobody," I answer quickly. "Who are you?"

"I'm not telling you, so just spit it out. What do you want? If you're thinking about robbing the place, there's nothing of value inside."

While that may be true materially, I can't help but admire her for trying to deter me from the baby I'm certain must be inside.

"I'm not here to rob you," I assure her.

"Okay, well, either stop acting like a creepy bastard or I'm going to call the police," she drops the bag of trash and jogs back up the porch steps toward the front door while simultaneously reaching for her cell phone from the front pocket of her hoodie.

"Wait!" I tell her. "No need to call the police." Pulling out my wallet, I take out all the cash I have on me, a little over two-hundred dollars and hold it out to her. "Will you just take this and hide it in the house someplace Naomi will find it?"

"How do you...are you a friend of Naomi's or something?" she asks as she takes a hesitant step in my direction. She pauses, not coming close enough to grab the cash.

"Not exactly," I mutter. "You the babysitter?"

She eyes me up and down and then looks back toward the house. "Oh! I bet you're Honey's daddy!"

"The baby's name is Honey?" I ask in surprise.

"Answer my question, and then I'll answer yours," she huffs.

"Fine. Maybe I'm her dad," I tell her.

"Gotta be more than a maybe if you're hanging around stalking her from the shadows."

"So her name is Honey?" I ask again, ignoring her observation.

"Yes."

Is it a coincidence that Naomi named her after the nickname I always called her? I highly doubt it. Does that mean she's forgiven me for getting her pregnant and putting her through a hellish labor? The last I heard at the hospital, she hated me and wanted me dead.

"What's her last name?" I inquire. I go over to pick up the bag of trash to take it the rest of the way to the can at the end of the sidewalk. Before grabbing it, I toss the cash in my hand down on the closest step. And holy hell, the garbage smells like something horrible rotted to death inside.

"Huh?" the girl asks in confusion.

"What's the baby's last name?"

"I'm pretty sure it's Dawson, like Naomi's," she responds. "Why?"

"Just wondering."

"What's your name?" she asks.

"Doesn't matter," I say when I turn to leave with the abomination in a bag. The words have barely left my mouth before I hear the snap of a camera. Looking back over my shoulder, I find the girl with her phone raised in front of her face and then it snaps again.

"I bet Naomi will recognize you. I'll just send it to her at work..."

"Don't!" I exclaim.

"Why not?" she asks with her eyebrow lifted in question.

"Because...I need to talk to her first," I hedge.

"Are you going to talk to her right now?"

"Yeah, fine. I'll go right now," I say, giving in to a teenage girl's demands because I've waited around long enough. It's time to man up and set shit right, even if it's going to be an uphill battle, and even if it means finally letting go of my pride.

∽

Naomi

"Can I get y'all anything else?" I ask my last table, four high school or college kids who finished eating an hour ago but have stuck around talking and laughing.

Oh, to be young again. I get it, I do, but my feet hurt, and I really want to get home to my baby girl. If I hurry, I may get to see her before she goes down for the night. Not that she'll sleep for more than three hours, but still. I was supposed to be on the nightshift, but Nancy is giving me shorter hours during the day because of all the late-night feedings.

"Nah, we're good," one of the guys at the table says.

While I wait them out, I go back behind the counter to start filling up ketchup bottles until I get to leave. Only, as soon as the kids stand up to go, another customer comes in – one with wavy, shoulder-length brown hair, wearing jeans and a leather jacket.

Fucking great.

It only takes Malcolm a minute to spot me, and then he's coming over, climbing up on one of the stools at the counter.

The sight of him sends butterflies soaring around my belly despite the fact that he's a complete and total asshole who doesn't deserve to look so good.

Clearing my throat and taking a deep breath to try and slow down my racing heart that's also doing somersaults in my chest, I keep my eyes focused on the ketchup bottles when I tell him as calmly as possible, "I don't know what you're doing here; but I need this job, so you and your foul temper need to leave."

My words may have sounded calm, but my hands are shaking so badly I have to put the ketchup bottle down before I drop it. How long has it been since I've seen Malcolm? Eight or nine months now? It's been almost a year, and yet just the sight of him still gets under my skin worse than I thought possible. Time made me forget just how handsome he is. I could've done without that unnecessary reminder.

My pulse pounds in my ears so loudly, I'm not sure I could hear Malcolm over it even if he did speak, but he doesn't. The entire time I avoid looking at him but can feel his eyes on me, burning me up as he drinks me in.

Finally, after what feels like years, his deep, rumbly smoker's voice says, "You never told me what the money was for."

And that voice...so demanding and rough, somehow hits me the hardest right between the legs. Then, his words sink in, and I go from hot and horny to annoyed in a second flat. Why is it always about money with this grumpy bastard?

Not a hi, how are you, good to see you, you're looking tired and exhausted. Nope. He gets straight to what's most important in his mind – money.

Sighing, I ask, "Could you maybe be more specific? What money are you talking about, Malcolm?"

"The money you owed your father and tried to steal from me."

Oh, *that* money. The money that cost me my self-respect, my dignity, my heart...

"What does it matter now?" I ask in confusion.

"It just does. Tell me," he demands, still as bossy as before.

"Fine," I huff. "I needed it to buy my grandparents' house after my Gram died."

"That shithole you currently live in?" he grunts his disapproval.

"It's not a shit – wait, why am I even wasting my breath discussing this with you?" I ask in outrage. "It's none of your business where I live!"

"Just answer the fucking question," Malcolm mutters, still as impatient and foul-mouthed as ever.

"Yes, the house I now live in used to be my grandparents'."

"Why save it when it obviously needs a lot of work?" he asks.

"Cosmetically, sure, it needs to be painted and a few things repaired, but none of that matters to me. The happy memories I had there with the only family I've ever known is what I care about. And that's what I want for..."

"That's what you want for what?" Malcolm snaps when I pause.

Grabbing a rag, just to have something to do with my hands and something to focus on besides his handsome face, I tell him, "The happy memories are what I want for my daughter too, more so than a nicer, more expensive house that's cold and unhappy."

"I thought she was *our* daughter," his deep voice rumbles over me like thunder.

"No, she is *my* daughter!" I yell at him while I scrub the counter so hard I may peel off the paint. "I carried her inside of me for almost nine months. I gave birth to her after six agonizing hours where I felt like I was being tortured, and I love her and care for her and-and provide for her, so she is mine and mine alone!"

"Why haven't you taken me to court yet?" he asks. "You could get enough cash from me in child support so that you wouldn't have to work here while some kid who doesn't look old enough to drive babysits our little girl."

Wow, so he's been to the house recently if he knows that Nancy's daughter Beth is my sitter.

"I told you I don't want your money," I remind him. "I would rather Honey grow up without a father than know you're hers and that you don't want her."

"That's pretty fucked up, don't you think?" he asks.

"No, I *don't* think so."

"Then how about this, how fucked up is it that after a year, an entire fucking year, I haven't been with another woman because I can't get you out of my goddamn head?"

He's...what?

"Like I would ever believe that for a second," I reply. "I saw the half-naked women at your house the day I came by to tell you I was pregnant. Are you really trying to pretend like you didn't sleep with one or all of them, and then half the female population in Carolina Beach over the last few months?"

"I haven't," he grits out, green eyes blazing with the kind of heat that dares me to call him a liar again.

"Even if you're telling the truth, that-that's not my fault," I say. I don't believe that Malcolm Hyde has been celibate for a second.

"Yeah, Naomi, it is," he argues. "And I'm sick and tired of missing you and wondering if I was wrong about you. I feel like... like an idiot, because I'm pretty sure I was wrong for thinking the worst about you."

"Yeah, you were. Took you long enough," I tell him as my chin trembles and throat burns from trying to fight back tears.

"I've just been burnt so many times before when it comes to people screwing me for money. After a while, it becomes harder and harder to trust people."

"I know," I reply. "You don't want to look like a fool again."

"Right," he agrees. "And lately, I constantly feel like a fucking fool for letting you go instead of giving you the benefit of the doubt."

"You are a fool," I tell him as tears burn my eyes because he's here, telling me the things I've wanted to hear from him for so long, since the night I left his house.

"So, what's it going to take for you to give me another chance?" he asks.

"Another chance?" I repeat in confusion.

"Yeah, to be with you, to meet my daughter."

"You want to meet her?" I say in surprise while losing the battle with holding back tears.

"I really do," he says. "She looks like you."

"You've seen her?"

"Yes. Not up close, but…she's beautiful, and I think she deserves to have a father in her life. Even if he is a fool half the time."

"*Most* of the time," I correct.

"Fine. Most of the time. I think I can be better for her, though."

"Oh yeah?" I ask.

"Yeah. I think I can be better for you too, Naomi."

God, I hate the way he says my name, making all of my anger and hate melt away like butter. "Why haven't you been with anyone else, Malcolm?"

"I dunno," he says as he leans onto the counter and runs his fingers through the front of his hair that's even longer than before. "Maybe because I didn't want to knock anyone else up on accident, but probably because I missed you and knew there wasn't another woman alive that I would fight my own brother to have."

"How is Fiasco?" I ask, causing Malcolm to instantly narrow his eyes at me.

"When I told him you were pregnant, he panicked because he thought it might be his," he admits.

"No, he did not! We never even..."

"I know," Malcolm mutters.

"So why would he..."

"Believe me, I know!" he says with a hint of a smile curving the corners of his lips. "And I don't need to hear the reminder of what you did with him that doesn't make babies."

"He may not be the brightest, but the man is *very* well-endowed."

"Why did you feel the need to go there and tell me that shit?" he grits out.

"Because you deserve it," I tell him. "You were an asshole, Malcolm. So don't think that one conversation after months is going to change things after what you put me through..."

Malcolm suddenly stands up and reaches across the counter to grab two handfuls of the hair on either side of my head. Before I know what's happening, he's crushing his mouth to mine, cutting off any words I was planning to say abruptly. His tongue invades roughly, demanding entry from my lips and taking what it wants, a swipe of my tongue, without asking, which is the epitome of Malcolm. I really wish I didn't get turned on by this sort of treatment. But I do, unfortunately.

I don't even realize that I'm kissing him back until he groans into my mouth. That's when I finally find the strength to peel his fingers from my hair and take two steps backward, out of his reach.

"You-you need to leave," I tell him, swiping my knuckles across my damp lips to dry them off. "I have to, um, get everything done so I can go home."

"I'll wait here until you're ready to leave," Malcolm tells me, taking a seat on the stool again.

"You're not coming home with me tonight," I warn him. I'm too off-kilter to have him in my house, especially near a bed. I could end up doing things that I regret tomorrow, if not immediately at the time they happen. Not to mention I'm not supposed to be engaging in any sexual activity before my six-week checkup.

Not that I'm thinking about sleeping with Malcolm.

I won't do that again.

Probably.

"Fine," he huffs. "Let me come over tomorrow so I can see the baby?"

"No. I'll, um, I'll bring her to your place."

"My place?" he asks.

"Yeah, your place. Say around four, before you go to work?"

"Fine." He forces the single word out like the place and time is not of his preference but knows there's not a lot he can do about it.

He's such a control freak, and I really do enjoy being able to throw him off balance any way I can. Serves him right for coming in here out of the blue and turning my world upside down.

CHAPTER TWENTY-SEVEN

Malcolm

I'm up at ten a.m. the next morning, cleaning my house like a maniac in preparation for Naomi and the baby to come over later.

Honey. My daughter's name is Honey. *My daughter.*

I don't think I've ever been so excited about anything in my life. At least, I think this feeling gnawing its way through me is excitement. It could be abject terror, as both emotions are not really in my normal repertoire. Whatever this new sensation is, it's driving my body into frantic motion, and my hands are so dry the skin is cracking from all the Clorox I've been using to wipe down everything, even the ceiling of my bathroom.

Once I've moved all the furniture searching for any sort of debris, and wiped down every exposed surface repeatedly, I stop and force myself to calm down. This seemingly inexhaustible energy feels like it might be the precursor to some sort of anxiety attack, and the last thing I need to do before Naomi and Honey come over is collapse.

I lean back and close my eyes, trying to focus on my memories with Naomi, and will my thoughts towards reconciliation. What can I possibly say, what can I possibly do, to try to fix things with her and prove to her that I want...that I want everything the two of them have to offer?

∽

Naomi

"Are you feeling okay?" Nancy asks at the beginning of my shift.

"Yeah, why do you ask?"

"Girl, you're shaking like a leaf. How do you plan to serve coffee like this?"

"Sorry," I say as I clasp my trembling hands together and wring them, ordering them to behave. "This afternoon I'm taking Honey to Malcolm's house."

"He's the biker who knocked you up and fled the scene?" she asks.

"Yes, pretty much."

"Is that the same guy who came by the house yesterday when Beth was there?"

"Probably."

"She showed me his picture. He's good-looking."

"Yeah, he is," I agree with a grin.

"Hard to forget a man that big and menacing with long, brown hair," she goes on to say. "Which is why I distinctly remember seeing him at the hospital..."

"What? When?"

"The day the baby was born."

"No, that's impossible. Yesterday was the first time Malcolm and I have spoken in months."

"Well, he was definitely there, right outside your room. I didn't know who he was there for at the time, but now…"

"He was at the hospital. You're sure?"

"Yes. And Beth said he drives a black and yellow bike that I bet looks a lot like the one that's always at the gas station across the street."

"Really? You've seen a black and yellow bike across the street?"

"You haven't noticed?"

"I guess I've been busy…" I trail off as I try to make sense of what Nancy's telling me. Malcolm was at the hospital when I was in labor, and his bike is always across the street? Has he been checking up on me all this time without me knowing it?

"Mind if I take a quick break?" I ask her, knowing she won't care.

"Sure."

"Thanks," I say while removing my apron. "I'm just gonna run across the road to talk to Greg."

"Okay. Get those shaking hands under control while you're gone too!" she calls out as I head for the door.

There's not much traffic on the two-lane road this morning; so as soon as it's clear, I rush across the pavement and across the parking lot to the door of the gas station.

"How's it going, Naomi?" Greg ask from behind the counter as soon as I walk in. "Looks like you had the baby!"

"I did, and I'm good, thanks. But I do have a question for you," I start when I walk up to the register.

"Okay?" he asks.

"Do you know Malcolm Hyde?"

"Uh-huh."

"How well do you know him?"

"Pretty well."

"Could you elaborate?" I ask.

"He comes in here most days."

"Most days?"

"Just between us?" he leans forward on his elbows to ask.

"Of course."

"The dude is in here all the time, usually once a day."

"And what does he do when he's here?"

Now Greg just blinks silently at me. "Greg?"

"He watches you," he finally says. "But not in a creepy way! Well, maybe it is sort of creepy. Mostly I think he's just been worried about you and the baby."

"I don't understand..."

"Not much to understand," he says. "The man obviously loves you and wants you back."

"He told you that?"

"Pretty much. He's just been trying to figure out how to go about getting you back after he fucked up."

"That's what he said? That he fucked things up with me?"

"Yep. Almost verbatim."

"Well at least he's an *honest* stalker."

"You're not mad at him for keeping an eye on you, are you?" he questions.

"I don't know," I say on a sigh.

"From what I know about Malcolm, he's not someone who enjoys admitting when he's wrong."

"No, he definitely does not."

"So you should probably give him a break. Or not! Totally up to you!"

"You have no idea what he's put me through," I tell him.

"Maybe not. But he does miss you. And he hates that you're working again so soon after having the baby. He's worried about you, Naomi."

"The grumpy bastard has a crazy way of showing it," I say with a shake of my head.

"Yeah, he does. And he's been so grumpy that he has to pay me for running off customers while he's here stalking you."

"He pays you to watch me from here?"

"Yep. Which is why I've been giving you free gas. It's the least I can do for all the money he's giving me."

"Now it's all starting to make sense," I mutter to myself.

After months of being angry at Malcolm and missing him, it blows my mind to think that he may have felt the exact same way about me.

CHAPTER TWENTY-EIGHT

Malcolm

"You came," I say in surprise after the doorbell rings and I open it to find Naomi on the other side.

"Yep, I came," she replies before I notice the baby seat thing she's carrying that's so heavy she's leaning to the side.

"Here. Let me take that," I tell her as I reach for the handle of the seat.

"Careful!" she warns me, refusing to let go.

"I'm not going to swing her around in the air upside down or anything," I assure her.

"How am I supposed to know that, Malcolm?" Naomi asks, before finally releasing her hold and letting me take control of the heavy seat. "You told me to get an abortion, and then you forgot all about us until yesterday! Or at least I *thought* you had forgotten us, but maybe you didn't..."

"I don't know what you're talking about," I say as I avoid her gaze, staring down at the sleeping angel instead. She's still just as tiny and beautiful as the day she was born.

"Yes, you do," Naomi challenges. "Greg told me everything."

"I'm gonna kick that traitor's ass," I threaten.

"No, you're not."

"Guess we'll see," I tell her even though we both know I'm full of shit. The fact is, Naomi and the kid have made me soft. I'm not sure how I feel about that yet. I do know that anything is better than being miserable and lonely.

"We can go sit in the living room," I say as I start in that direction.

"I hope you've sanitized since your party," I hear Naomi mutter under her breath.

"No naked women have been inside since then," I confirm.

I take a seat in one of the black leather recliners and place the baby seat down on the floor in front of me while Naomi hesitantly lowers her ass down on the sofa.

"So, can I hold her or what?" I ask before I undo the strappy things crisscrossing over the baby to yank her out.

"Not yet. You can't wake a sleeping baby. Are you crazy?"

"Occasionally," I answer truthfully. "What are we supposed to do until she wakes up?"

"Wait," Naomi responds, leaning back a little further on the sofa.

"Okay."

I have no fucking clue what to say to her. *How have you been* is a ridiculous question since she knows that I already know how she's been – shitty. I refuse to resort to small talk about the weather; and talking about the MC will only result in talking about Fiasco, which I would rather avoid.

"I need a smoke," I mutter mostly to myself.

"Of course you do," Naomi huffs. "But you're not smoking around her."

"I know that." How dumb does she think I am? "I've actually cut back to less than a pack a day, which is why I need one."

"That's good, I guess," she replies, sounding less than impressed.

And to tell the truth, I have no goddamn idea how to impress this woman anymore, if I ever even did. She liked my dick and my tongue well enough months ago and just tolerated the rest of me.

"What are we doing here, Malcolm?" Naomi finally asks, getting straight to the point.

"I don't know," I tell her truthfully. "I wanted to see you and the baby."

"You *just* wanted to see us?"

"Yes. I just wanted to see you and talk to you, and here you are, which makes me think you want the same damn thing."

"We're not going to sleep together again," she says flatly.

"Sleeping wasn't what I had in mind for you when I get you back into my bed," I joke, which doesn't go over well when Naomi rolls her eyes and gets to her feet. "Sit your ass down, honey. I was joking! Mostly." She glares at me. "Sit! Please?" Finally, she does what I asked. "We already know we're good together in bed. Maybe I want to try and see if we could be good together out of it too."

"I have no idea what that means," she huffs.

"It means what I just said!" I tell her. "Trying to move on and forget you didn't work. I don't want to be without you anymore. Or the kid."

"Why should I trust you?" she asks without looking at me. "You didn't trust me, and you hurt me..."

"I told you I'm sorry. Or at least I apologized to you in my head a million times. Either way, I'm sorry, Naomi. I fucking miss you. Hell, I even miss the kid, and this is the first time I've ever seen her."

"I'm not sure if you're good for her yet," she admits softly. "She's innocent and fragile; and if I can help it, I'm not going to let anyone ever hurt her."

"Good. That's good," I tell her. "I don't want anyone to hurt her either. Or you. And I know I'm asking a lot of you to trust me on this; but at the same time, I think you always wished you had a dad around, just like I did."

"I never wanted Harry around," she argues. "But yes, the idea of a father figure, I longed for it as a kid. Every Christmas I asked Santa for a father, not toys. What I got with Harry wasn't what I had in mind."

"Tell me about it," I mutter. "My mother used to love telling me how I could never be a good boy because of what my father said about me. He told her I was *born of sin* and didn't stand a chance at ever being a decent human being."

"What do you mean?" Naomi asks.

"My father was not only a married man but also a man of god. He knocked up my nineteen-year-old mother one morning on a pew right in the middle of his church before Sunday school."

"Holy crap. How do you know all of that?"

"She told me. Several times, unfortunately. And she said he blamed her for dressing so slutty and being a tease. Told her it was her fault he gave in to temptation even though he was the one with a wedding band on his finger."

"What an asshole."

"Yeah. I never met him because she didn't just like to tell me the story of how I was made. She also liked to repeat the fact that my father paid her five hundred dollars to get an abortion when she told him she was pregnant. But since she thought she could get more cash out of him if she had me, she didn't go through with it. He sent her a few hundred dollars a month to keep her quiet, so that his wife, and a few years later, their son, wouldn't find out about me, his bastard first born."

"Jesus, Malcolm," Naomi whispers.

"I've never told anyone that before," I admit. "And the reason I'm telling you now is not because I want your sympathy. I don't. I was fine without that fucker in my life. But I don't want to ever be anything like him. I never should've blamed you for getting pregnant or offered you money to end it. It was my fault for not putting on a rubber, not yours. I'm finally able to take responsibility for that, something my father never did."

"No, you trusted me, and I let you down. I never meant to..." she starts and then gets choked up.

"I know. So how about we just forget it and move on? Start over, even though I know it won't be easy and that I have a lot of work to do to try and make it up to you and to Honey."

"That...that sounds good to me," she agrees with a half-smile that I've missed like crazy. "I missed you, even when I didn't want to."

The breath I didn't even know I had been holding comes pouring out in relief.

∼

Naomi

Our visit with Malcolm is actually going better than I anticipated. He's being...nice and sweet, which is unexpected. He even came right out and said he misses me, *us*, and wants another chance...

"She's awake!" he says so suddenly that Honey fusses. "Sorry."

"It's okay," I say as I get up from my seat to unbuckle her and lift her out of the car seat. "Still want to hold her?"

"Yeah," he replies, so I place her in his arms and take a step back.

In true Malcolm fashion, he doesn't dare ask me to confirm if he's holding her right. He just acts like he's done it a million times before. And he's actually good at it too, cradling her and protecting her in his strong, tattooed arms. This may be the first time he's actually held her, but already I can tell that he's falling in love and wouldn't let anyone hurt her.

"Now I get why you looked so happy in the hospital even though you were crying and had been in so much pain," he says softly. Guess Nancy was right about Malcolm being at the hospital after all which is... surprising.

"I can't even remember the pain now," I admit. "Once I saw her, it was like it all disappeared. I was just happy my daughter had come into the world healthy. Holding her made me feel whole. And before that moment, I didn't know if I could be a mother. But those doubts went out the window because I knew I would do anything for her."

"Yeah," Malcolm agrees as he stares down at her.

I hate admitting that he's even hotter holding our daughter. It's not fair. I'm not prepared for the onset of new emotions that bombard me, pushing aside some of my anger and resentment toward him. Some, but not all, by any means.

A few minutes later, when Malcolm finally looks up at me, he asks, "Do you need anything?"

Is that a trick question? What I *needed* months ago was for him to not be a dick and push me away. I needed *him*, not his money, and I sure as hell didn't need his insults.

"No, Malcolm, *we* don't need anything from you."

"Don't be like that," he says. "You may not want my help, but you need it. You needed it months ago when you told me you were having my kid, but I failed you back then. Let me try to make it up to you now. At least let me hire some guys to fix your air conditioning and make sure the house you two live in doesn't fall down around you."

"The house is fine."

"Yeah, well, fine isn't good enough for me. I would sleep easier if I knew it was safe."

"Sleep? What's that?" I joke. "All I get are naps, no more than two or three hours."

"The babysitter doesn't help?" he asks.

"Beth is there with Honey while I'm at work, but I'm her mother. It's my responsibility to get up with her all hours of the night."

"If I were there, I could help."

A bark of laughter escapes me. "You wouldn't last a night!"

"Try me," he says, face serious.

"I'm not leaving her with you overnight!"

"I didn't ask you to," he replies. "I'm telling you to let me stay at your place at night."

Of course he *tells* me and doesn't ask. "That would be too much right now," I tell him. "I need you to give me some time and take things slow."

"I don't know how to go slow," Malcolm says. "But I'll try to learn how for you."

"Okay then," I agree, even though I'm not entirely sure what I'm agreeing to.

All I know is that it sounds like Malcolm genuinely wants to be with me and Honey. His reassuring words are one thing, although I'm not sure I'll buy anything he says until he backs up his words with his actions.

CHAPTER TWENTY-NINE

Malcolm

"First order of business," I tell my brothers who have gathered around our table in the Dirty Aces chapel. "I want to thank all of you for putting up with me these last few months. I know I've been an asshole and that this has been a difficult time, what with two successful mergers, and the deal we have with that fat prick Harry. I didn't make shit easier with the Naomi drama."

"Ah, shit, prez, that's all behind us now," Fiasco scoffs.

"Well, maybe not as far behind as you might think," I say as I size up everyone at the table. "I remember how everyone reacted when I told you Naomi ended up pregnant. I've thought a lot about it these past few months, and she and I have decided to try and give it another go, for the sake of our daughter."

"Really?" Silas scoffs. "You need to just buckle down and pay your monthlies, like Fiasco here, and put that whole situation behind you."

"I knew you would feel that way," I nod to Silas. "And some of you, or hell, all of you may agree. But it's not your decision who I'm with, and it won't affect my ability to lead the MC. This isn't a club matter. It's my fucking life. Naomi won't be working for us, and she won't have anything to do with our business. This is just between us. You know I wasn't right in the head for a while, and a big part of that was because she wasn't around. I'm not going to sit at this table and talk about my feelings to you sons-of-bitches, so let's just leave it at that. Now I know I want to be with her, and that's how it's going to be. I expect you to treat her like any other ol' lady when she's around, and to respect our relationship. Other than that, you can feel any damned way you want about it. Sound good to everyone?"

"Yeah," Devlin says.

"Of course," Wirth agrees.

"Do what you want," Silas snorts. "I said my piece."

"It's all cool with me, too, prez," Fiasco nods. "I am over all that drama, and don't even want to look back. I'm thinking with my head, just like you said."

"That's good to hear," Nash says with a grin. "I'm on board with this too, Malcolm. To be honest, seeing how close you two were when you were together, I couldn't help but feel a bit jealous. I had something like that once a long time ago with my ol' lady, and the truth is I still miss her."

"Oh, for fuck's sake," Silas gripes. "Don't we have anything else to discuss before one of us gets our period?"

"Hell yes, we do," I confirm with a smile. "We've got three more clubs to consider for a patch over, and I want to go over our future plans for profiting off our relationship with Naomi's fat dipshit father. I've had some time to get things straight in my head, brothers, and I think you're going to like what I've got planned. I think you're going to like it a lot."

"We going to piss the fucker off?" Fiasco grunts.

"Hell, or at least make some decent money?" Devlin asks.

"There will be plenty of both things, boys. I'm talking enough money to keep everyone's pockets nice and full. My idea is to keep building up a tight working relationship with Harry's speed supplier and then eventually convince them to cut out the fat middleman, which means all of Harry's profit would be ours."

"You wanna screw him over, blindside his business after he gets comfortable?" Nash asks with a smirk.

"Let's just say that we are gonna do him dirty."

"Here! Here!" the guys all shout their agreement.

EPILOGUE

Malcolm

A few months later...

When Naomi gets back from shopping, she has to stop her car out on the main road, as the driveway leading up to her old farmhouse is full of big trucks from the contractors I called.

"What is all this?" she asks me as I open the door to her old rust-bucket for her, leaning down to steal a kiss.

"This is the crew that is going to put some shine back on this creaky, old house of yours, so the city doesn't end up condemning it." I grin down at her before helping her out of the car. "How is my Honey-Bear doing back there?" I ask as I lean back into the car, getting a smile and a coo from my daughter, who is gleefully trying to devour a squeaky giraffe.

"Dammit, Malcolm," Naomi huffs. "You didn't have to do all this, spend all this money on me and Honey. And you could have at least consulted with me about the changes before doing them!"

"What makes you think I'm doing it for you two?" I ask her in mock surprise. "No, no, these boys are here to install a man-cave for me. If I'm going to be hanging around this rickety old farmhouse, I need a place to get away from all the racket you two make."

That gets a smile out of her; and I know that once she's grinning, the battle is already won.

"What are they really doing, Malcolm? Tell me the truth," she sighs.

"I'm serious, they're fixing the place up. Not with a man-cave; though, now that I think about it, that's not a bad idea. Naomi, this place needs serious repairs for our daughter before she starts crawling and walking! You know I'm right."

"What happened to *if you're going to be spending more time here?*" she asks me with an arched eyebrow.

"Well, I mean, when you're ready for us to take that next step. I'm not trying to rush you after everything..." I stammer a bit before she bursts into laughter.

"Grab Honey, you big jackass, and then help me get these groceries inside. I'll make dinner tonight if you'll promise to stay. Deal?"

"You want me to stay? I mean, if you're ready for me to sleep over...." I trail off as she laughs at me again.

"Yes, Malcolm, I'm more than ready. Honestly, I've been ready for quite some time. I was just waiting for you to get your swagger back and pin me to a wall or throw me on the bed. You really have been taking things slow, trying hard to do everything right, haven't you?"

"Yeah, I really have," I agree sincerely, because I've never wanted anything more than Naomi and Honey.

"Well, let's get one thing straight then," Naomi says around two bags of groceries. "Pinning me to a wall or throwing me on the bed is now, officially, perfectly okay. Do you understand now, Mr. President?"

"Oh, I understand, honey," I agree. "Come on, Honey-Bear, let's get inside and get you settled down. Your mother and I have some very serious catching up to do tonight."

"You bet your ass we do," Naomi agrees. "You have no idea how bad it got while I was pregnant. Those hormones will drive you out of your damned mind."

"Speaking of driving people out of their minds," I grin at her as we struggle up the stairs with the groceries and the baby. "I should probably talk to you about what these guys are doing to our house. Oh, and um, maybe give you a few details about the plan I'm working on for your dear old dad."

"Please tell me you're finally going to be karma driving a Mack truck and mowing that horrible man down," she says when we make our way into the kitchen where she sits our groceries down and I lower Honey's car seat.

"Don't worry. We are going to make Grandpa Harry a very, very unhappy man," I tell her.

"In that case, you, Malcolm Hyde, have made me a very, very happy mama," Naomi says when she winds her arms around my neck and kisses me.

"There's something else in my pocket that might make you happy," I tell her.

"Ooh, kind of hard to miss that," she says when she grinds herself on my cock.

"Not that. Well, not just that," I amend before I reach down and pull her repaired necklace out and dangle it from the tip of my finger.

"My necklace!" she exclaims when she snatches it up. "I thought you may have thrown it in the trash!"

"Fuck that," I huff. "Do you have any idea how much those diamonds are worth?"

"Diamonds?" Naomi gasps as she brings the locket closer to her eyes. "No way! I thought they were cheap gemstones. The yellow and black are..."

"Both diamonds."

"Wow, Malcolm, you really shouldn't have," she says as she unhooks the clasp to put it around her neck. "And I mean, you really, really shouldn't have."

"You're the first woman I've ever bought a diamond for, and I want you to be the last," I say when I grab her hips to pull her body flush with mine.

Brushing her lips over mine, she asks, "Are you asking me to be your old lady?"

"Honey, I'm asking you to be my old lady, my wife, my every-fucking-thing. So what do you say?"

"I say...you've got yourself a deal, Mr. President," Naomi says, lifting a weight off of my shoulders.

"About. Fucking. Time," I mutter between quick kisses before I throw in some tongue action, kissing her so hard her knees go weak and my arms are the only thing keeping her steady.

The End

COMING SOON

Thank you so much for reading Malcolm!

Devlin's book is up next in the Dirty Aces MC series.

Order your copy: https://mybook.to/DirtyAcesDevlin

~ Synopsis ~

As one of the enforcers for the Dirty Aces, sometimes I have to hurt people. Using my fists to get results is not something I enjoy – it's just part of the job. My loyalty will always be to the MC and no one else.

So just because Jetta James is a hot as hell girl I once hooked up with at a rock concert, it doesn't mean I can give her brother a break on the gambling debt he owes to the Aces.

When Jetta finds out I'm a member of the MC, she thinks I'm bad news; but her brother Sean is the one drowning in his bad decisions.

And the day Sean makes a stupid deal that puts Jetta's life in danger, I'll beat, maim, and kill every asshole who stands in my way in order to save her, even her own brother.

Order your copy now: https://mybook.to/DirtyAcesDevlin

ABOUT THE AUTHORS

New York Times bestselling author Lane Hart and husband D.B. West were both born and raised in North Carolina. They still live in the south with their two daughters and enjoy spending the summers on the beach and watching football in the fall.

Connect with D.B.:
Twitter: https://twitter.com/AuthorDBWest
Facebook: https://www.facebook.com/authordbwest/
Website: http://www.dbwestbooks.com
Email: dbwestauthor@outlook.com

Connect with Lane:
Twitter: https://twitter.com/WritingfromHart
Facebook: http://www.facebook.com/lanehartbooks
Instagram: https://www.instagram.com/authorlanehart/
Website: http://www.lanehartbooks.com
Email: lane.hart@hotmail.com

Join Lane's Facebook group to read books before they're released,

ABOUT THE AUTHORS

help choose covers, character names, and titles of books! https://www.facebook.com/groups/bookboyfriendswanted/

Find all of Lane's books on her Amazon author page!

Sign up for Lane and DB's newsletter to get updates on new releases and freebies!

Printed in Great Britain
by Amazon